DECADENCE

By the Authors

Ronica Black

In Too Deep

Deeper

Wild Abandon

Hearts Aflame

Flesh and Bone

The Seeker

Chasing Love

Conquest

Wholehearted

The Midnight Room

Snow Angel

The Practitioner

Freedom to Love

Under Her Wing

Private Passion

Dark Euphoria

The Last Seduction

Olivia's Awakening

A Love That Leads to Home

Passion's Sweet Surrender

A Turn of Fate

Watching Over Her

The Business of Pleasure

Something to Talk About

Decadence:
Passionate Pursuance

Renee Roman

Epicurean Delights

Stroke of Fate

Hard Body

Where the Lies Hide

Bonded Love

Body Language

Hot Days, Heated Nights

Escorted

Glass and Stone

Desires Unleashed

Decadence: Redemption

Piper Jordan

Hotel Fantasy

Decadence: Exclusive Content

Writing as Toni Logan

Share the Moon

The Marriage Masquerade

Gia's Gems

Perfectly Matched

DECADENCE

by
Ronica Black, Renee Roman
and Piper Jordan

2023

DECADENCE

ISBN 13: 978-1-63679-361-0

THIS TRADE PAPERBACK ORIGINAL IS PUBLISHED BY
BOLD STROKES BOOKS, INC.
P.O. BOX 249
VALLEY FALLS, NY 12185

FIRST EDITION: AUGUST 2023

CREDITS

EDITOR: CINDY CRESAP
PRODUCTION DESIGN: STACIA SEAMAN
COVER DESIGN BY TAMMY SEIDICK

DECADENCE

PASSIONATE PURSUANCE

Ronica Black

CHAPTER ONE

Emory Bennet startled as the driver's side door opened and her partner, DeAngelo Vargus, slid in with two cups of coffee in his hands.

"Smells good," Emory said, her voice gravelly from a long night of zero sleep. She took the offered coffee and inhaled.

"It tastes like shit," DeAngelo said, slurping loudly from his own cup as he yanked the door to the unmarked cruiser closed.

"Yeah, well, we can't all run on Dunkin'."

He snorted, obviously amused.

"Any movement?" he asked.

Emory eyed the apartment complex across the street as she sipped her hot coffee. "Nada."

DeAngelo checked the clock on the dash. "I wish they'd freakin' hurry it up."

"I have a feeling they'll be sleeping most of the day after the party they had last night."

"Gino won't. Not if he's got business to tend to."

"True that. But still, when it comes to his girlfriend, his rules and routine tend to fly out the window."

"Speaking of flying out the window," DeAngelo said as he eased his down, "this really tastes like shit." He dumped his coffee and crinkled the cup to toss at her feet.

"Hey!" she said, feigning offense.

"It was empty!"

"Still!"

He laughed again and then snapped his fingers at her as if something had just popped into his mind. "Speaking of which! What about that girl of yours? What's her name? Candy?"

She narrowed her eyes at him. "Cadence."

"Right. How's she doing?"

"She's doing fine, thanks."

"You meet her yet?"

"Now, when would I have had time to do that?"

"I don't know." He studied her closely and then refocused on Gino's gaudy tricked-out Hummer across the street. He was a newer criminal, a young wannabe drug runner, and it showed in everything he owned and wore. "You at least FaceTime with her yet?"

"No."

"Ha! She's a catfish. I knew it."

"She is not. We're both just really busy. And I don't know. I'm…"

"Don't even say shy. That's a load of bullshit."

"Not shy, but more reserved."

"You're chicken shit."

"That too."

"What, you worried she won't like you?"

Emory shrugged. "I'm worried that this great chemistry that we have might not come through on FaceTime. That it will all be over."

He rubbed his stubbled jaw. "I can see that."

"We've put in a lot of time via text and phone calls, and I just don't want the magic to end."

"Well, you've got to meet her sometime."

As if out of habit, Emory checked her phone. There were no texts from Cadence. She'd told her she was going on a stakeout, and Cadence always seemed to respect her work boundaries. It was one of the things she liked most about her. She wasn't clingy.

"She wants me to go to Vegas to meet up with her."

DeAngelo swung his head around. "No shit?"

Emory nodded.

He nudged her. "Then go, girl. God knows you need to get away."

Emory sighed. "It would be nice."

"But you don't want the magic to end."

"No, I don't."

"So go and find out. At least you'll know. And if you're worried about the magic, then plan some things. Take her out, rock her world."

Emory considered it. Cadence had told her some interesting things about herself. Like how, thanks to some serious bad luck with two previous exes, she was pretty much a novice when it came to love, sex, and romance. If Emory put her mind to it, she could really plan some things that would blow her mind. That is, *if* Cadence would let her. Cadence seemed to be all about giving. Would she allow her to blow her mind?

Maybe if it's a surprise she won't have a chance to shy away.

Her stomach tightened as butterflies let loose at the possibility.

"Hey, you know, that's not a bad idea."

"I rarely have bad ideas," DeAngelo said.

He nudged her playfully but kept his focus across the street.

"Oh, hold tight, here we go," he said as he secured his seat belt. His dark eyes were trained through the windshield at the couple moving across the apartment complex parking lot.

"Fuck. He's got a duffel bag." Emory placed her coffee in the cup holder, secured her own seat belt, and readied herself for the pursuit. She slid on her sunglasses and fingered her Glock on her belt. "He got any backup?"

"Doesn't look like it."

"What's that about?" They watched Gino, a skinny kid with long limbs and oversized clothes, climb into his black Hummer with the black duffel bag and lean over to kiss his girlfriend.

"I don't know," DeAngelo said. "Could be because it's so early."

He started the car and eased out of the parking space, careful to crawl onto the main road a ways behind Gino and his girlfriend.

"What? Drug runners can't get up early?" Emory laughed.

"Kids this young? It's not their favorite thing to do."

Emory grabbed her coffee and took another hearty sip. DeAngelo was right, the coffee was bad, but at the moment she didn't care. She just wanted the heavy caffeine. They'd been on stakeout overnight watching Gino at a party, waiting for him to make his move. Originally, they'd thought the drop might happen at the party, while Gino was inside. Someone just dropping the drugs off inside his vehicle and then walking away. But they'd watched the Hummer all night and there had been no movement.

Now, with a duffel bag in sight, they were in business.

"He's gonna make the run with his girlfriend in tow? What a nice, thoughtful boyfriend to use her as cover."

"He's not that smart," DeAngelo said.

"No, but the guys he's doing business with are." Gino was a runt, a newbie. The latest to be used for runs by a well-known drug cartel. But he was young, and not very bright. He'd proven that when he was selling on the street corner. For whatever reason, however, the cartel was upping his game, giving him a chance. Maybe they saw something in him she and DeAngelo didn't.

They braked and followed Gino to the left down Grand Avenue.

Instinctively, Emory checked her mirrors, making sure they weren't being followed. She didn't see anything suspicious.

"It's too quiet," she said.

DeAngelo checked his mirrors. "You think they're on to us?"

"Could be. Maybe we should hang back."

DeAngelo slowed and they fell farther behind the Hummer. But no one appeared to be following. Eventually, Gino pulled into a local donut shop and parked. They pulled in across the street and settled in.

"Guess you were wrong about running on Dunkin'," DeAngelo said.

"Ha."

Gino and his girl climbed out and headed inside.

"Did you notice that?" Emory asked.

"Yep. He didn't set the alarm on the Hummer."

"No, he did not."

"And he did not take the duffel bag."

They sat in silence. Waiting. Then, as if on cue, two men walked out of the donut shop and climbed into the Hummer. They started the engine.

"Shit, they're taking the vehicle."

DeAngelo cranked the car and Emory called for backup.

They pulled out onto the street behind the Hummer, just as Gino and his girl emerged from the donut shop and crawled into a Chevy Caprice.

"They're using the cars to make the exchange."

"Yep."

"What about Gino?" He was turning the opposite direction in the Caprice.

"We'll have to get him another time. Right now, we follow the Hummer and the duffel bag we've seen."

"Shit, D. I really wanted Gino." She glanced behind them, looking for the Caprice. "He's bad news, I just know it."

"I agree."

She shifted in her seat and lifted her shirt to adjust the strap on her bulletproof vest. Just then the call came in for them to follow but not engage. They needed to wait for backup.

"Bet you're thinking about Vegas now," DeAngelo said with a smirk. "It must sound pretty good."

"It is sounding better and better."

He laughed and accelerated, then nearly slammed on the

brakes as the Hummer braked hard and turned into a full-service car wash.

"What the hell?" Emory said, readying her weapon.

"There!" DeAngelo pointed at the Hummer as a garage door to the car wash opened and a man came out directing the Hummer inside.

"Fuck, we're gonna lose sight."

DeAngelo parked at the edge of the car wash, and they watched helplessly as the garage door closed.

"Uh, I think we better forget the exchange," DeAngelo said.

Emory blinked, unsure if what she was seeing was real. Four men were walking quickly toward them from the outskirts of the garage. One untucked his T-shirt, showing off his prominent handgun.

"Go, go, go!" Emory said, aiming her weapon.

DeAngelo put the car in drive and swung around to head toward the exit. Shots rang out behind them as they squealed out onto the street. Emory ducked and reported the situation as bits of glass bit into their skin from the back window.

DeAngelo slammed on the gas, fishtailed, and then steadied as they sped down the road. Emory checked behind them, found only civilians, and then looked ahead to see four oncoming squad cars, lights blazing, sirens blaring.

"We got backup!" Emory said.

DeAngelo checked the mirrors, then did a U-turn and fell in behind the squad cars.

"Here we go," he said as they neared the now chaotic car wash. He glanced over at her quickly and gave her his all-too-famous devious smile.

"You ready for Vegas now, chica?"

Emory swallowed against a dry throat and a thudding heart.

"Yeah, man. I'm definitely ready for a trip to Vegas now."

Let's just hope I can make it there in one piece.

Chapter Two

"Oh, my God. Girl, this looks so good. I look so good."

Cadence Macord lowered her friend Rodney's salon chair and smiled at him in the mirror.

"You look fabulous," she said.

"And you are the one who made it all happen." Rodney leaned forward, turning his head from side to side. "Damn, I'm pretty."

Cadence laughed. "You certainly are."

"I knew I wanted the blue, but I have to admit, I was a little worried about how it would turn out. But damn, it's so good!" He fluffed his shoulder-length hair and grinned.

"The blue brings out your eyes," Cadence said, removing his cape.

"And what gorgeous eyes they are," he said, batting his lashes. He stood from the chair and leaned in to kiss her on both cheeks. "You truly are a color specialist, my dear. The best damn one in Vegas and probably the Western Hemisphere."

"I don't know about that," she said, feeling a blush coming on.

"Nonsense! I know of what I speak. Right, ladies?" He did a turn for the other women in the salon and curtsied at their whistles and praise. "Cadence is the best colorist this side of the Mississippi."

"I must say, I agree," Janet said, coming up to kiss Rodney good-bye. "Why do you think I struggle to keep her in my salon?"

"Well, do what you have to! I want her to stay," Rodney said.

He handed Cadence a folded stack of cash and then blew her a kiss. "Thank you, love. Jeffrey's going to shit. I've got to get home to show him."

Cadence caught the kiss and blew one back. "Give him my love," she said. "And tell him he's due for a cut and color himself."

"Will do." Rodney waved good-bye to the rest of the salon and walked out the door as if he were on a catwalk.

"I so love that man," Cadence said, watching him go.

Janet laughed. "And he adores you." She squeezed her shoulder and offered a soft smile. "You really are the reason why we're so popular. The work you do in and out of the salon is top-notch, Cade. Truly."

"Thanks."

A Goldfrapp tune came from Cadence's pocket, and she quickly retrieved her phone. She knew, thanks to the tune, that the text was from Emory.

"Is that her?" Janet asked, leaning in to look at the screen. "Oh, it is! Go take a break and answer it. I'll check in your next client when they arrive."

"Thanks, but I'm done for the day."

She fumbled with her phone, anxious to see the text that had just come in. She hadn't heard from Emory in over twenty-four hours, and she was beginning to get concerned.

"Everything okay?" Janet asked, seeming to sense her unease.

"Huh? Yeah."

But the text had been vague. Asking for her to call Emory when she could get time alone.

She met Janet's gaze. "I'm gonna take off."

"Okay. See you tomorrow?"

Cadence nodded, her mind already solely on Emory.

She answered her text while she gathered her things and headed for the door.

Give me 20 mins. Hope everything is ok.

She said good-bye to the salon and stepped out into the heat of the May afternoon. She found her Mini Cooper and crawled inside, happy to sit in the warmth of the vehicle for a few moments.

She eyed her phone again, looking for some sort of response from Emory, but there was nothing.

"What could be going on?"

She started her engine and checked her mirrors. She noted that she looked tired, and she slipped on her shades to appease herself. She wondered, as she drove out of the parking lot, if Emory would find her attractive. It was something that had been on her mind a lot lately.

Initially, they'd traded photos after meeting on the dating app, but it was difficult to get a good read on someone's best filtered pics. She had sent pics from the year before, when her hair was streaked with purple. Now it was auburn with a few blond highlights, and she'd changed her makeup some too, wearing it brighter and heavier now.

"Will she like it?"

She'd suggested they FaceTime to catch up and at least meet that way, but Emory had discouraged it and she honestly hadn't fought that hard to change her mind. She just hoped Emory was for real and not some crazy catfish, using another person's photos to try to catch her.

She didn't think she was. She sounded too mature and too down-to-earth. She seemed to have a serious job as a detective, so maybe she just liked keeping her cards close to her vest.

A red light caused her to brake, and she switched on the stereo and tried to think of other things the rest of the ride home. When she arrived, she dodged the cats, grabbed a cold bottle of water from the fridge, and sank down on the couch. The cats joined her, already rubbing up against her in greeting.

"Not now, sillies," she said softly. "We'll eat when I get off the phone."

She sipped her water and sent Emory a text, letting her know she was home.

Seconds later, Goldfrapp announced her call and Cadence answered.

"I've been thinking of you all day," she said by way of greeting. A smile came, involuntarily, even though she was still concerned over her long period of no contact.

"Really?" Emory said. "You must be psychic."

Cadence chuckled, truly glad to hear her sexy voice. "Must be. Any idea why?"

"You tell me."

"Oh, I don't know. Could it be because I like you. Like you a lot?"

Emory laughed. "I hope so."

Cadence leaned forward, finally hearing some fatigue in her voice. "What's up? You don't sound quite like yourself."

Emory was silent. Cadence dodged a tall, curled tail in her face and gently shooed Penelope off her lap.

"Em?"

"Something happened yesterday."

Cadence stiffened. "What?"

"I was involved in a shooting."

"Oh, my God!"

"It's all right. I didn't get hurt."

"All right? Em, that's terrible." She stood and began to pace with her heart and mind racing. The cats retreated to the kitchen, where they began to meow and march around their food bowls.

"I'm okay. Honest."

"Jesus. What happened? How did it happen? Where did it happen? Are you sure you're okay?"

"I'll give the details a bit later. Right now I'm a bit drained from the interviewing I had to do at the station."

"Oh, my God," Cadence said again, retrieving a can of cat

food from the pantry. She filled Penelope's and Pedro's bowls to keep her hands busy. At the moment she didn't feel like she could sit still. She was too worked up.

Emory continued, obviously sensing her unease.

"My partner, DeAngelo, he's okay too. So are the other guys. But the suspects, they took some pretty hard hits."

"They did?"

"Yeah. Three are in the hospital."

"How many were there?"

"Six."

Cadence rubbed her forehead, her anxiety not quelling in the least. She rinsed the can, tossed it in the recycle bin, and then got busy wiping down the already clean counters.

"Cade, I really am okay."

"So you've said."

"But you're still upset, aren't you?"

"Em, I haven't even met you in person yet, and here you go and get shot at? Are you trying to give me a heart attack?"

Emory laughed.

"Hey, you knew I was a cop."

"I thought it sounded sexy."

They both laughed.

"Yeah, I look real sexy right now all huddled in my blanket on the couch."

"Aww, I bet you do."

Emory fell silent. Cadence waited patiently, knowing how seriously stressed she must still be.

"Something good did come out of it, though," she finally said.

"Oh?"

"I've decided to take some time off to come to Vegas to meet you."

Cadence felt her entire body warm. "I hope you're serious because my skin just caught fire with those words."

"It did, huh?"

"Uh-huh."

"I'd like to be there for that."

"Then get yourself on a plane, sister."

"I plan on it."

"When shall I expect you?"

"When do you want me?"

"Ha, is that a trick question?"

Emory laughed again.

Cadence leaned back and examined the calendar hanging on the fridge, and her heart beat with excitement.

"Can you come next week?"

"I don't see why not."

"Good. Because I have an idea."

"Why do you sound so mischievous?"

"Oh, I don't know. Maybe because I am at heart."

"Yeah?"

"Mm-hmm."

"What did you have in mind?"

"I have a friend who is throwing a masquerade ball for women only at her mansion on Saturday. And I think it would be fun if we met for the first time at that party, wearing masks."

"Ah, I see."

"What do you think?"

"I'm not sure. I've never been to a masquerade before."

"Yeah, well, this isn't just any masquerade. It's an erotic masquerade."

"Come again?"

Cadence chuckled. "It's one of those parties where anything goes. Particularly sex."

"You're kidding."

"I'm not, I swear. My friend Elizabeth Hathaway puts it on every year, and every lesbian in America tries for an invitation."

"And you got one?"

"I did indeed. One for me and a guest."

"Sounds a little risqué from what I know about you."

"Hey, I can handle it. Besides, my focus will solely be on you."

"It will, eh?"

"So, what do you say? You want to arrive separately wearing masks and meet up that way? And then after that, well, anything goes."

Emory exhaled long and slow. "I don't know, Cade. Will a cop like me fit in?"

"Women from all walks of life attend. Lawyers, doctors, cops, CEOs. And there's security."

"Wow."

"That's what makes it so fun. You don't know who you're talking to. Everyone remains anonymous."

Emory was silent again.

"You can't tell me you aren't the least bit curious?" Cadence asked, returning to the couch.

"Mmm, you may have my interest."

"May have?"

"Do you really want to go?"

"To meet up with you? More than anything."

"Then I'm on board."

"Really?"

"As long as you're truly up for it."

"I am."

"Then I think, my dear, that you've got yourself a date."

CHAPTER THREE

"Coming!" Emory removed her cat from her chest and crawled from the couch as the doorbell rang for a second time. "Who in the hell is it?" It was after ten and she had been seconds away from binge-watching *Breaking Bad* for a third time.

She hurried to the door, checked the peephole, and haphazardly smoothed down her wrinkled Arizona State T-shirt and plaid pajama bottoms. Then she unlocked the door and pulled it open to face DeAngelo full on.

"What the fuck?" she asked as he stood staring at her with a wide grin.

He held up a couple of bags. "I brought Ah-So."

She rolled her eyes. "That's not always going to work, you know."

She pushed the door open and allowed him entry. He breezed by her and headed straight for the coffee table.

"Maria working the late shift tonight?" Emory asked.

"No, she's home. She's just sick of me."

"Huh. Imagine that." Emory went into the kitchen to retrieve plates and bowls and then returned to help him fish out the food. It smelled delicious, even if he was using it as a bribe to come bother her for hours on end.

He straightened and rubbed his hands together. "Got any beer?"

"Mmm." She plucked a bite of noodles and DeAngelo crossed to the fridge and returned with two cold Corona Premiers.

They sat on the couch and dug in, Roscoe the cat long gone. Emory could see him hovering near the bedroom door. He didn't like company. He was a highly antisocial kitty.

"So, what brings you by?" she asked, taking a bite.

"Gino," he said as he chewed.

"Oh, yeah?"

"His buddies gave him up. In fact, they were more than happy to. Seems he was expendable."

"Not surprising."

"Nope."

"We pick him up yet?"

"Yep. He's crying like a baby. Doesn't want to do time."

"Jesus."

They each took another bite and sipped their beer.

"So, how you holding up?" De Angelo asked.

She shrugged. "Okay, I guess. You?"

"I'm all right."

"How's Maria taking it?"

"She didn't let me out of her sight until about an hour ago."

"Ah."

He pointed his chopsticks at her. "I tell you what, Em. I went straight home and hugged my damn kids until they pleaded for mercy."

She laughed. "I can imagine."

They ate some more and he tilted his head at her. "You should have a family, Em. Someone to come home to."

"I have the kitty."

"You mean the little asshole?"

"He can hear you, you know."

"No, but seriously. You should have someone. You deserve that."

"I'm okay."

"You're not, but I won't argue with you."

"Thank you."

DeAngelo stared at the silent television. "You're watching that again?"

"I was about to."

"Christ, you need a life. You're supposed to come home to relax, not watch things pertaining to work on TV. Come on, Em. You know this."

"I just happen to like that show. It's well done."

"Even so."

She sipped her beer and decided to cheer him up with a change in subject.

"I've decided to use my time off to go to Vegas."

He perked up. "No kidding?"

"I'm going to meet Cadence."

He smiled. "Now you're talking."

"I leave Friday and I'm nervous as hell."

"Fighting criminals you're fine, but meeting a woman for the first time and you're scared shitless."

"That about sums it up."

He shook his head. "She's going to love you. And even if she doesn't, then it wasn't meant to be. Just look at it like that."

"Thanks." She chewed some more and then swallowed. "We're meeting at a masquerade ball."

He looked at her and wiped his mouth with a paper napkin. She continued.

"Everyone wears a mask and is anonymous. We've decided to go separately to see if we can find each other. Oh, and I guess it's a rather risqué endeavor. Women only. Lots of sex."

"Sounds kinky."

"Mm-hmm."

"I'm surprised you're going. You can be as antisocial as Roscoe."

"I can not." She laughed despite herself. "Anyway, I figure

why not? Could be fun." She wriggled her eyebrows. "In fact, with a little planning on my part, it could be a lot of fun."

He took another bite but seemed less than impressed.

"You don't think so?"

"I don't know. Sounds kind of *Eyes Wide Shut* to me. And you know I'm not a big Stanley Kubrick fan."

"It's supposed to be fun. Not dark."

"I hope for your sake it is."

"I thought you'd be excited for me." She set down her beer and wiped her mouth.

"I am. I'm just…I wish Maria and I could get away."

"The shooting got to you more than you're letting on, huh?"

He nodded. "I keep thinking of those perps walking toward us. I keep hearing the back window pop and I can feel the glass hitting me."

"I know."

"It was close, Em. Too close."

She reached out and touched his arm. "What else?" She knew there was more. She could feel it coming off him like an invisible mist.

"The perp I shot. He's not doing so well."

"Oh, no."

He set down his chopsticks and finished his beer.

"I'm sorry, DeAngelo. That can be tough."

"It's a mixed bag of feelings, isn't it? Shit, why can't I be heartless?"

"Because you're one of the good guys, my friend."

She leaned into him and nudged him. "And I happen to love you for it."

He returned the nudge. "Love you too, Em."

They leaned on each other for a long moment before Em eyed the television once again. "What do you say to kicking back to watch season one of *Breaking Bad* again?"

"And get a first-rate chemistry lesson on how to make meth? Sure, why not?"

She laughed softly and grabbed the remote. Then they both sat back and propped their feet up on the coffee table and readied themselves for a long night of binge-watching some other cop's make-believe problem.

CHAPTER FOUR

S o, what's she like?" Geneviere asked, resting her chin in her hands. They were sitting inside at the Boulder Dam Brewing Company, enjoying drinks and an appetizer, along with numerous other locals who wanted a good drink and equally good conversation on an increasingly hot day.

Cadence couldn't help but smile, glad that she was getting to see her longtime friend after many months, but also glad that Geneviere was asking about Emory. "Emory? Well, let's see. She's kind, thoughtful, funny—"

"Skip the nice bullshit. Is she hot?"

Cadence sipped her drink, a rattlesnake bite, which consisted of hard cider and the brewery's Powder Monkey pilsner. She tried to suppress a grin.

"I knew it! She's smokin', isn't she?"

"She's pretty hot."

"Let me see." Geneviere snatched her phone just as Cadence found the three pics of Emory.

"Oh, damn. She's a looker." Geneviere wriggled her eyebrows as she studied the pics. "That's it? Only three pics?"

"Yes." Cadence grabbed her phone. "That's all I need."

"Please, oh, please tell me you have video-chatted with her."

Cadence lowered her gaze and stared at Emory on her phone. She was in Sedona with the red rocks behind her, her thick dark mane pulled back in a ponytail. Sunglasses were covering her eyes.

"I don't need to," Cadence said.

"Cade! Those pics could be of anyone. Not to mention the fact that there are only three, and they aren't really representative of real life, are they?"

"They're good enough." She liked the pics. Looked at them every chance she got. So what if one wasn't very detailed. The other two were. Kind of.

Geneviere sighed and drank her Ocho Loco IPA. Cadence took advantage of the silence and spoke.

"It doesn't matter, because I'm going to meet her this weekend anyway."

"Seriously?"

"Yes."

"'Bout time. What's it been, months?"

"Since you first left for Egypt."

"Damn. So, seven months?"

"Uh-huh."

Geneviere took a bite of the nachos and chewed. "Well, it certainly feels good to be home."

"How was your trip, by the way?"

"The same. If you've done it once, you've done it a thousand times."

"Said Indiana Jones."

Geneviere laughed.

"Yeah, your life is so boring," Cadence added.

"It is better than most, I'll agree to that."

Geneviere was an archaeologist and she got to travel the world. Cadence was often envious.

"You can come with me sometime. You're always welcome."

"I'd be bored."

Geneviere raised an eyebrow. "Yeah, I can see how one would get bored in Egypt."

Emory shook her head. "You'd be busy and I'd be bored at the dig."

"You could explore. You know, see Egypt while I worked."

"What's the fun in that?"

"God, you need a woman. Someone who can go places and explore sights with you."

"That would be nice."

"So, you think this Emory might be the one?"

"I don't know. Maybe." *I hope so.*

"Does she like to travel?"

"I think so."

"Good."

"She's often very busy, though. She's a detective."

"Oh. Wow. That can be rough."

"How do you mean?"

"Rough hours, rough job in general. She doesn't exactly get to see the best in people. And people don't exactly roll out the welcome wagon for her either."

"I never thought of it like that." She stared into her drink, feeling for Emory. "She was actually in a shoot-out last week."

"No way!"

"She didn't get hurt or anything, but I think it scared her. Scared me."

Geneviere reached across the table and placed her hand on hers. "Cade. Be sure this is something you want, okay? Being with someone who has a job like that…it can be stressful."

"So I'm learning."

"Besides, isn't she all serious and shit? Most cops are."

Cadence smiled. "She can be. But she's agreed to meet me at Elizabeth Hathaway's party."

"Shut up! There's no way your girl knows what all that means. No way. Otherwise she wouldn't agree to go."

"She surprised me too."

"Well, did you tell her what all goes on?"

"I did."

"And she still agreed?"

"I think she really wants to go. Her life sort of flashed before her eyes, so to speak. And well, she said if I really want to go, then so did she."

"That makes sense. After the shoot-out and all. But don't be surprised if she tucks tail and runs."

"Hopefully, I'll find her before she can take off."

"Oh, that's right. The masks." She clapped. "This just got super exciting. I wish I could go."

The waitress brought them another drink and asked if they'd like to order a meal. Cadence politely declined. Geneviere did the same.

She held up her beer. "Here's hoping your girl's not a total stick in the mud."

Cadence laughed but clanked her glass, silently wishing the same.

❖

Cadence pressed the call button and relaxed back against her couch. She closed her eyes, still feeling warm from the three rattlesnake bites she had at the pub. Normally, she didn't drink so much, but it had been good to see Geneviere and she'd started to melt with desire when they'd began discussing Emory. Now she was home and calling her, hoping she wasn't going to disturb her.

"Hi," Emory answered with her usual sultry voice. It sent shock waves of heat right through Cadence's body.

"Hi back."

"I was just thinking of you."

"Were you?"

"Oh, yes. Thinking about how you said you wanted to completely spoil me while I'm there."

"I do. I don't want you to have to worry about a thing. I just want you to relax."

"Well, you know it's not in my nature to relinquish control so easily."

"I figured as much. But truly, while you're here, I hope you do. At least for a little while."

"Mmm, I might can make do. For you, that is."

"Thank you."

"What exactly did you have in mind?"

Cadence thought for a moment. "I don't know, long massages, long walks, long nights."

"Wow, that sounds really good."

"I hope it does. Because I can't wait to do it all with you. For you."

"It doesn't all have to be about me, you know."

"No, but I think it should. Seeing as what you went through and all. This trip will hopefully be a big stress reliever for you."

"It will be. Whether you spoil me or not."

They sat in silence for a moment. Then Emory spoke.

"I would love to get a chance to spoil you too, Cade."

"Maybe next trip."

Emory laughed. "So, that's a no?"

"I just want to focus on you."

"You're adorable."

"I'm smitten is what I am." Cadence yawned, unable to stop herself.

"Go get some rest," Emory said softly.

"But you leave for Vegas in the morning. I won't get to talk to you again before we meet."

"That's what you wanted, isn't it?"

"Yes. But—did you get the invitation I mailed you? You need that to get into the party."

"I got it."

"And you need a mask."

"Got that too."

"And there's no cell phones allowed, so—"

"Cadence, it's okay. I'm prepared."

"Should you need anything, I told my friend Elizabeth to keep an eye out for you. So if you need anything at all, go up to the jellyfish bar and give them your name."

"The jellyfish bar?"

"You'll see."

"And you mean your friend Elizabeth Hathaway?"

"Yes. She'll have someone available to help you."

"Sounds like you've got it all planned."

"I'm trying to."

"I think you need to relax now, silly," Emory said. "Everything will be fine."

"It will. I know."

"Okay then. I'll see you Saturday evening."

"Okay. See you then."

"Good-bye."

Cadence kissed the phone. "Good-bye."

Chapter Five

Emory sat on her bed in the Cosmopolitan and ran her fingers over the black feathered mask she'd bought for the masquerade. She'd asked a good friend to make it for her, and Stella had done a beautiful job. The black feathers were so dark they reflected the light and gave off hues of blues and deep purples. She couldn't take her eyes off it, and she just knew the mask would go great with her outfit.

Her phone chimed and she set the mask down on the bed and checked her texts. It was Cadence. She was reminding her that she'd sent a car for her to get to the masquerade. Emory smiled and texted back. Cadence was really pulling out all the stops for this party. It was obvious she was anxious about showing her a good time.

"If she only knew," Emory said, placing the phone on the nightstand. She stood and stretched in front of the large window overlooking the lights of Vegas. The sun was just setting, and the night was coming on like a beautiful dark demon in the desert. Her heart thudded as she thought about tackling that demon and riding it like a black stallion into the moonlight. She wanted Cadence at her back, arms wrapped around her tightly. Now it was time to make that happen.

She stripped and crossed to the bathroom for a long, hot shower. She soaped herself thoroughly and then rinsed and applied scented lotion. Then she applied the accompanying cologne and got dressed.

Her panties and bra matched, and they were as black as the feathers on her mask. Her slacks were also black and fitted with a pleat down the middle. She buttoned them and then shrugged into her white dress shirt and buttoned that up. The shirt was also fitted, and she rolled up the sleeves to her elbows and then fastened on the black leather suspenders and made sure to fasten the strap that went across her chest as well. She checked herself in the mirror and straightened out the wrinkles and left her shirt unbuttoned about halfway up, making sure to show off a wink of her bra. Then she fastened her necklace around her neck, the one with the platinum padlock charm on it. It was a good luck piece, and tonight she needed some luck.

She grabbed her comb and ran it through her wet hair. Her waves were dark and thick, so she pulled them back into a tight ponytail. She knew her hair would be a dead giveaway, but it really wouldn't matter. Not by the time Cadence saw her, that is.

She lightly applied some makeup, accenting her eyes and her full lips. Then she strapped on her heavy-looking watch with the black leather band and eyed the time. She crossed to the bed and slid into her expensive black loafers and reached for her mask. As it rested on her lap, she grabbed her phone and sent one last text.

Smiling, she didn't wait for a response, and she stood as her hotel phone rang.

"Yes?"

"Madam, your driver has arrived."

"Thank you."

She hung up, gave herself one last glance, and headed for the door.

It was time to catch the demon.

CHAPTER SIX

Cadence crossed her bare legs in the back of the limo and tried to take a deep breath. But her nerves were getting the better of her, and her heart rate kicked up as they slowed at the gate to gain entry to Elizabeth's party. She smoothed her hands over her short, dark red minidress and pressed her lips together, hoping her lipstick was still fresh and colorful as she wondered for the hundredth time what Emory would be wearing.

"No matter what, I'm sure she'll look hot."

She sipped her chilled white wine and looked through the window at the lights on the driveway that lit up as they drove upon them. Elizabeth lived like a queen, and frankly no one deserved to more than she did. She'd grown up an only child to exceptionally wealthy parents who completely ignored her. She'd been allowed no friends, no childhood really. Now Elizabeth was making up for that tenfold. She had dozens of good friends and threw herself into her charity work, changing the lives of hundreds on a yearly basis. She was beloved and rightfully so. Elizabeth was good people, and Cadence was glad she knew her.

The limo, which Elizabeth had insisted on providing for her, slowed as they came to the circular drive in front of the house. Cadence stared in awe, just as she often did when she came to visit Elizabeth. But tonight it was double awe. Lights accented the mansion and the foliage, and there was a giant projection of the word *Decadence* catching everyone's eye.

"She really went all out."

The limo driver must've been equally awed because the car behind them honked to get her to pull up. She did so and put the car in park. Then she climbed out and helped Cadence out with a shaky hand.

"Ma'am," she said.

"Thank you."

The driver tilted her hat at her and a woman came up and took her hand.

"Welcome to Decadence Masquerade Ball. Right this way."

Cadence tried to speak but nothing came out.

The woman, who was extremely well endowed, had on a button-down shirt with two slits in it that showed off her nipples. To top it off, her nipples were pierced with bars, and they held the shirt in place. Cadence had never seen anything like it.

"You might want to put this on," the woman said. She took Cadence's mask and held it up for her.

"Oh, right." She fumbled with it, but the woman quickly helped her, stilling Cadence's hands.

"There," she said, stepping back. "You look magnificent."

Cadence smiled.

"Good enough to eat," the woman said, leaning into her ear.

Cadence felt herself blush, and she fingered the white and red feathers of her mask.

"You better get in there before I have you all for myself." The woman winked at her from behind her Zorro-style mask. "My name is Ruby. Find me should you...need anything."

Cadence nodded, somewhat dumbfounded. In her peripheral vision, she saw her limo drive away and another vehicle pull up. Ruby helped snap her from her trance by giving her hand one last squeeze before she dropped it to go help the next guest. Cadence took her cue to follow the other women ahead of her up to the door.

Another woman, dressed similarly to Ruby, smiled at her and waved her up the stone stairs.

"Welcome to the Decadence Masquerade Ball. My name is Shelly. May I have your invitation, please?" she asked.

Cadence handed her the fancy black envelope she'd received in the mail and nervously glanced around as Shelly scanned the QR code of the inner card. Then she smiled and welcomed her further inside.

The distant beat of the music grew louder as they entered, and Cadence had to squint to make sense of the once familiar layout due to the dim lighting. But by the time she was all the way in, her eyes had adjusted, as had her ears, and she felt her heart thudding in her chest with excitement. It was like walking into a massive nightclub.

"This way," Shelly said, taking her by the hand.

"Where are we going?" Cadence asked, a little confused.

"To the bar."

They headed toward the source of the music, to the right of the massive staircase, walking quickly across the marbled floor. Cadence kept looking around, trying to take everything in.

"Which one?" She half chuckled, a little amused at herself.

"The big one," Shelly called back. "The jellyfish bar."

Shelly stopped and spread her arms wide, showing off the enormous tank, lit up by black light, in which numerous beautiful jellyfish swam. A bartender smiled at them and nodded to Shelly that she'd take it from there.

"What can I get you?"

"I have no idea," Cadence said, still staring in awe. She'd been to the mansion before, but had never seen it done up like this.

"It's something else, isn't it?"

"You said it."

"Ms. Hathaway has exquisite taste."

"That she does."

The bartender slid her a drink. "Rum and Coke."

"How did you—"

"Oh, darling please. You aren't hard to peg," someone said, coming up from behind.

Cadence turned, a little startled, but then recognized the woman immediately as her longtime friend.

"Elizabeth."

"You mean you can tell it's me?"

"Well, I've known you for years."

"It's the hair, isn't it? The cut and the salt-and-pepper give me away every time. I ought to let you color it."

She smiled and her turquoise eyes gleamed behind her mask. She grabbed Cadence's drink and handed it to her.

Cadence sipped it and turned with Elizabeth to overlook the crowd. Outside, through the open doors, women were swimming and shrieking with joy, while others made out in the large Jacuzzi.

"Your home looks—damn, Elizabeth, it's incredible," Cadence said, still in awe.

"Thank you."

"I—" She shook her head.

"You're wondering why you've never been here on masquerade night?"

"No, I—"

Elizabeth waved her off. "As you know I'm a very gracious person, a selfless person, but I do like my privacy most of the time. This party I throw every year is just a way to give back to the lesbian community. To give them a safe place to go all out and be themselves for one night only. And as for you, I wanted to get to know you on a personal level before I invited you to the party. I've done that with all my close friends."

"I can see that."

Elizabeth laughed. "You've only just arrived. You haven't seen anything yet."

Elizabeth studied her for a long moment before she spoke

again. "You know, Cadence, we've known each other for quite a while now. Ever since that charity event at the Bellagio for victims of domestic violence. You remember. The one where I actually let you do my hair."

Cadence nodded. "I'll never forget it. We made those women feel so good. It was such an honor getting them all ready for that big dinner."

"You donated your skills and talent, and I donated the gowns and the finances."

"It was quite the success."

"It was, wasn't it? Anyway, my point is that we go back some years now and I've never ever seen you with anyone special."

Cadence blinked, a little surprised.

"Oh, I assume you've dated. But other than that, nothing… serious."

"You'd be correct."

Elizabeth smiled. "Which brings me to tonight. You mentioned when you called me that you'd be meeting someone special here tonight."

Cadence sighed as she glanced around. "I don't think, in retrospect, that it was such a good idea. I don't know how on earth I'm ever going to find her."

"Well, let's just say that I'm here to help you with that very issue."

"You are?"

"Of course. I can't let a good friend like you down now, can I?"

"I don't understand."

"That's okay. You don't have to."

Elizabeth handed her a card. This one in a velvety red envelope.

"What's this?"

Elizabeth leaned in. "The ticket to finding your girl."

Cadence felt her eyes widen.

"Oh, yes, darling. She's here. And she's waiting. Question is, can you find her?"

And with that Elizabeth Hathaway gave her a wink and walked away.

CHAPTER SEVEN

Cadence stared down at the card and then looked at the bartender, who only smiled and wiped the bar.

"Is she serious?"

The bartender mimicked zipping her mouth closed and headed for the other end of the bar.

"How can this be? Elizabeth doesn't even know Emory."

She quickly fumbled with the envelope and opened up the black satin finish of the card. In bold, cursive letters, it read,

Tonight all your wildest dreams will come true, if you'll let them.

Come to the room in the back for a risqué dance, if you're game.

Love,

Emory

What the hell? How had—? What the—?

"What is going on?"

But no one was near enough to hear her, and the beat, which she could've sworn had grown louder, began to thump in her chest, luring her onward.

She returned the card to the envelope and made her way around the bar to the back end of the house. The beat seemed to resonate from there, and she grew excited as she realized she was about to meet Emory face-to-face for the first time.

What a way to meet. This little ruse involving Elizabeth was genius. And here she'd thought she was the one who would be pulling all the strings during Emory's visit.

Wrong.

Somehow, Emory had beat her to the punch.

God, this was hot.

She came upon a back room, where the beat thrummed like a giant heart in its rib cage. Red lights scarcely lit up the dark. The floor seemed to vibrate, as did the walls, but her ears did not hurt, for the beat was too deep, too methodical, too fucking primal. She entered and stood very still, letting her eyes adjust. Everywhere she looked, masked women danced, stuck to each other like glue. Some still had their clothes on, some did not. And some looked to be in stages in-between.

Cadence stood like a statue, heart in her throat. And then suddenly there was someone at her side. She turned, expecting to lock eyes with Emory. But the eyes appeared green and the woman blond. She had a devilish smile, the kind that could lure even the most stoic of individuals.

Cadence started to speak as the woman reached out and ran a fingertip down her bare arm.

"Shh," she said, shushing her with her other hand. She held her fingers to Cadence's lips.

"Would you like to dance?"

Cadence swallowed. "Uh, I'm actually looking for someone. She's—"

The woman lowered her hands to trace the outline of Cadence's body as Cadence continued to speak.

"You see—I'm looking for her."

"I know," she said.

"You do?"

The woman smiled. "Of course. She sent me to you."

"She did?"

"Uh-huh."

"But—"

The woman took half a step back and slowly, oh so slowly,

lifted her miniskirt up on one side to show a red velvety envelope tucked into a black lace garter belt.

"See?" she said, lowering her skirt. "You dance with me, you get the next card."

Cadence swallowed again, her mind and body both reacting to what she'd just seen and heard.

"I—"

"Would you like to dance?"

Cadence glanced around and saw that no one else was paying her any mind.

"I'm not sure."

The woman laughed. "Emory wants you to, you know. She wants you to relax and let go. Think you can do that if you know she's watching you?"

She stepped in and tugged Cadence tightly to her.

"What do you say?"

"I—uh—really wanted Emory."

"I bet you do," the woman said. "But Emory, like I said, Emory likes to watch."

"She—likes to watch?"

"Mm-hmm. Which is where I come in."

"You mean she's watching you and me right now?"

"Yes. So we'd better give her a good show, don't you think?"

Cadence stared at the woman for a moment and then hastily looked around at the others. But with the red lighting and the pulsating bodies and masks, she knew she'd never find Emory without further help. So she nodded. "Okay."

"Very good." The woman pulled Cadence even tighter and clung to her, wrapping her leg around her, making sure to grind her warm center against Cadence's thigh.

"Oh, fuck yeah," she let out as she began to gyrate.

They moved to the rhythm of the low, guttural beat. Cadence held the woman tight and thrust her own body into hers, while closing her eyes and thinking of Emory, thinking of Emory watching her.

Around them, sweaty bodies welcomed them to the erotic dance of the heartbeat, and soon Cadence was swaying in that rib cage of a room, holding on firmly to the woman in front of her, rubbing herself against her, building a never-ending pressure up between her legs. The woman spoke in her ear, edging her on, talking dirty, trying to get her to the next level.

But she needn't have tried. Cadence was already there, just imagining Emory watching. So she put on her best show, dancing and grinding. She couldn't believe how determined she felt, how…dangerous. Anything to get to Emory.

"Harder," the woman said. She licked her neck and Cadence groaned.

"Faster," the woman said. She tried to back her up against the wall, next to another moaning couple. But Cadence held firm and then quickly turned them so the woman had her back to the wall.

She merely laughed in response. "Oh, hell yes, baby. Take me."

Cadence knotted her hair in her hand and tugged her head back, feeling wild and reckless.

"Fuck," the woman hissed. "You've got me so wet."

"Give me the card," Cadence whispered, voice tight with involuntary desire.

The woman gasped for air. "I can't. Not yet."

"When."

"When you…are pleasured."

"What does that mean?"

The woman opened her eyes. "It means that I must pleasure you first." She laughed. "Are you ready for that?"

Without warning, the woman placed her hands on Cadence's chest and spun them around so that Cadence was back against the wall.

Cadence watched helplessly as the woman lowered herself and hiked up her skirt, which Cadence tried to fight at first but soon found herself allowing to happen.

This is what Emory wants.

Next to them, two kissing women muttered, "Let her, let her take you."

Cadence closed her eyes as the beat overtook her and the hot breath of the woman tickled her thighs and then her satin-covered center. She shook as her body reacted, opening up like a blooming flower to let her in.

"Mmm," the woman said as she edged Cadence's panties aside. "Beautiful." Cadence gripped her head and panted down at her. Somewhere Emory was watching.

The woman stuck out her tongue and licked her, and in an instant nothing else mattered. Not Emory, not the woman, not anything. Only the beat.

Cadence grabbed her head and pulled her to her, insisting that she latch on. The woman laughed into her and began to feed. Cadence slammed her head back and clenched her eyes.

"Fuck," she groaned.

"Yeah," the couple next to her said. "Yeah, baby, take it."

Cadence blocked them out and whipped her head from side to side. She was wide open and sopping wet and the woman was feasting on her like she was her last meal. Cadence began to thrust into her, fucking her face. Around them more women moaned and groaned.

"Jesus," she growled.

The woman looked up at her and stopped for a split second only to breathe.

"You taste so good," she said.

Cadence massaged her head. "Good," she said and pulled her back to her to finish.

She glanced around the room, which now felt heavy with sweat and breath and desire. She looked at each woman, wondering if any of them were Emory. But she couldn't tell. All she knew was that the pressure was building between her legs. The sweet, sweet pressure creating its own beat now. Faster and bigger and hotter than ever before.

And suddenly Cadence couldn't get enough. She held the woman fast to her and fucked her furiously, any and all inhibitions gone. She began to call out.

"Emory, fucking yes, Emory. Are you watching? Can you see me?"

She slammed her head back and laughed. "I'm going to come for you now. You hear me? Emory?"

The woman held on for dear life as Cadence continued to fuck her and then at the last second, she pulled away, and Cadence nearly fell on wobbly legs.

"What the fuck?" Cadence managed.

The woman was as breathless as Cadence.

"That was some fuck," the woman said with a grin, adjusting her mask as she stood.

"But we didn't finish."

"We weren't supposed to." She leaned into her once again and spoke. "I was supposed to save the best bit, the last bit for Emory." She grinned.

Cadence smoothed down her skirt and touched her own face, trying to ground herself.

"You mean it was—"

"Fucking hot," the couple next to them said.

The woman laughed.

"It was pretty hot. You got really turned on."

"I was thinking of Emory," Cadence said, unamused.

"I know. I heard you. I think the whole room heard you."

Cadence blushed.

"You ready for your card now?"

She nodded.

The woman lifted her skirt and guided Cadence's hand up her leg to the garter. "There you go, hot stuff."

Cadence took the card and the woman whispered again.

"You know, Emory sure is a lucky woman." She backed away and winked at her. "See you around, sweetie." And she walked away.

Cadence, who was suddenly overwhelmed by the heavy feel to the air and the heavy, intrusive beat, hurriedly left the room and tore open the card.

There, in the same elegant writing as before, was another message.

Your pleasure was all mine.
Now it's time for you to call the shots.
Follow the lovers to the room of delights.

Chapter Eight

Cadence slowly lowered the card as a gentle hand covered hers. The couple that had been to her left was standing right next to her now, expectant looks on their faces.

"Come with us," the taller one said. She had hair as black as night, spiked with tips of blue. They matched her eyes, which were bright and seeking. They also matched her outfit, which was bright blue with sequins, fitted to her body like a second skin, with a mask striped like a zebra covering the upper part of her face.

"Yes," her companion said, leaning in to lick at the row of steel earrings studding her ear. "Come with us."

Cadence released the card as the shorter woman took it and tucked it in her bra. She was dressed opposite her lover, with a red sequined top and matching shorts glued to her body. Her mask, however, was the same as her woman's. Zebra striped. Her physique was curvy and thick with muscle. Her long brown hair was braided straight down the middle and hung loosely on her back. When she moved, every muscle seemed to coordinate and move with her, showing off her strength.

The blue-eyed woman caught Cadence staring as they exited the room.

"Ginger is beautiful, isn't she?"

Cadence hesitated, but then decided to be honest. After all, they'd just had an intimate encounter in front of one another and now she was being told to follow them. It was a little late for shyness.

"Her body is incredible."

"She's a gymnast." The woman smiled.

Cadence returned it. "Well, that explains it."

"You should see the things she can do."

I'd like to.

But Cadence merely fell into step next to her companion as Ginger split the crowd for them. They were leaving the heat of the beat behind them and zigzagging through the massive house to the other wing where a dark room, lit only in golds and oranges, awaited. As they entered, Cadence realized that the colors were due solely to flames. Rows of candles lit up the edges of the room, highlighting a big bed in the center.

Ginger stopped at the bed and turned to smile at her.

"This is it," she said. "Where our fun begins." She sat and ran her hand over the satin duvet, while her thigh muscles rippled beneath the skin of her crossed legs.

"Is it," Cadence said, growing nervous once again. She glanced around, looking for a camera, anything to understand how it was that Emory could see them. But she saw nothing. That was until a line of masked women entered the room, all of them standing behind the rows of candles, as silent as a dark, dark night.

"Raven." Ginger held out her hand to her lover, and the dark-haired woman crossed to her and took it. Then they both looked back at Cadence.

"It's time," Ginger said.

"Yes," Raven echoed.

"I don't understand," Cadence said.

"You're to instruct us," Raven said, reaching out to stroke Ginger's face.

Ginger caught her hand. "Not yet," she scolded her. "Not until she says so."

Cadence hurriedly scanned the room, searching for anyone who could possibly be Emory. But she could make out the features of no one. The dancing flames were playing tricks on her eyes.

"Instruct you?" Cadence said.

"Yes," Ginger said. "Tell us what to do."

Cadence blinked. In the distance, she heard the heartbeat of music. In her chest, she felt it, as if she were still there right next to it. Thud, thud, thud. Her skin flushed and she was back to full arousal once again. Behind her a woman, the last woman to enter the room, closed the door. Then she made her way to stand at the end of the row of women.

"Emory?" Cadence asked.

But the woman stood very still, looking straight ahead at the bed, just as the rest of them did.

"This is the voyeur's delight," Ginger said. "Only so many women are allowed to attend. And only one, that being you, is allowed to instruct."

Raven lifted her blue-sequined halter and revealed the next card.

"That is, if you want this."

Cadence felt her mouth water and her throat was dry. "I want it," she rasped. "I want Emory."

"Then you shall have her," Ginger said, plucking the card out to toss upon the bed. "Once you tell us what to do."

"And the others are here to watch?" Cadence asked.

"Precisely."

"Don't be shy, now," Raven said. "We're ready for you."

"More than ready," Ginger said. "Especially after the beat room."

Cadence swallowed. "I'm—not shy." She knew Emory was in the room somewhere. She just wished she could find her.

She fisted her hands and stiffened her wobbly legs. Her panties were soaked, and she was still more than turned on. If only Emory knew. If only she knew what all this was doing to her.

She does know.
It's why she's doing it.
God, this is hot.

"Kiss her," Cadence said, her voice firmer than she expected.

Raven stared at her with obvious surprise.

Cadence said it again. "Raven. Grab her by the nape of the neck and kiss her. Hard."

Raven grinned for a split second and then eased her hand along Ginger's jaw to the back of her neck. Then she dipped her head and kissed her. Hard.

Ginger moaned and Raven knelt to taste more of her. It was more than obvious the two had a deep attraction to one another.

"Now with tongue," Cadence said, stepping closer. Her gaze traveled the room. *Where are you, Emory?* But all the women remained stoic and quiet. Still as a preyed-upon mouse.

Raven complied and Cadence saw the flash of flesh dart out of her mouth and into Ginger's. Ginger answered with her own and she clung to her, tugging Raven closer.

"Straddle her," Cadence said. "Raven."

Raven straddled Ginger and the kissing continued.

"Kiss her good and hard," Cadence whispered. "Like it's the first time ever tasting her." She moved around the bed, walking slowly, searching for Emory. "Pretend it's the first time you ever tasted her, felt her, saw her. Devour her like you would under those circumstances."

Raven held her face and kissed her harder, groaning into her. Ginger fell limp in her arms and let her have her. Let her taste every last little bit.

Cadence watched the women, looked for the deep dark eyes she knew to be Emory's. But she couldn't tell them apart from all the others. The candles danced mischievously, keeping her in the dark when it came to Emory.

It was fucking driving her nuts.

"Now her neck," Cadence said, stopping to watch. She stood with her hands behind her back, her face as hard as a rock. This was her show, and she intended on giving a good one. Right in front of Emory.

Raven devoured Ginger's neck, causing her to cry out.

"Kiss and suck her skin," Cadence said.

Raven did.

"Now nibble it."

Raven did and Ginger cried out again and arched, offering more of herself. The movement caused Raven to groan again, and she feasted harder, nibbling up and down the sides of her neck.

"Now lick her. Lick her where you bit her."

Raven did.

Cadence watched for a long moment, mesmerized. Then she snapped out of it and went in for more.

"Ginger, remove her shirt."

Ginger blinked, trying to focus with Raven still at her neck. With unsteady hands, she began to unzip the halter from Raven's back, lowering the zipper one slow inch at a time before freeing it completely.

"Now toss it aside."

Ginger did.

"Raven, stop licking her and arch back so we can see you in the candlelight."

Raven flexed her toned back and torso for everyone to see. Her small breasts were taut and her nipples were tinted a dark brown, begging for touch.

"Ginger, touch her breasts," Cadence said. "But only skim her nipples."

Raven gasped as Ginger did so, careful to only lightly touch her nipples.

"That's it," Cadence said. "Make them hard. Make them beg for touch."

Raven struggled for breath as her body shook with the pleasure.

Cadence felt a twinge between her legs as she watched and she began to move again, walking the edges of the room.

"What should they do now?" she asked the women. "Hmm?" But no one answered. They only stared.

Cadence returned and faced the bed once again. "Lick them," she said. "Flick them with your tongue."

Ginger pulled her closer and did just that, extending her long, agile tongue to tease the tips of Raven's nipples, causing her to sigh and buck wildly.

"That's it," Cadence whispered, almost to herself, completely turned on. She turned to the row of women. "You see that, Emory? Is it turning you on?"

It is me. My God, where are you?

She faced the bed. "Now, take them in your mouth," she said.

Ginger eagerly took Raven's breasts in her mouth.

"Suck them."

She did.

"Ah, fuck," Raven rasped, clinging to her head.

"Suck them hard," Cadence said. "Fucking tug on them."

Ginger took them full on in her mouth and sucked them so hard she tugged on them. In and out and in and out.

Somewhere near the candles, a woman made a noise of desire. It caused Cadence to laugh wickedly.

"Glad we're getting to somebody besides me." She watched for a while longer as Ginger feasted and Raven groaned and grimaced from the intense pleasure. Her face had reddened and sweat beaded her chest and hairline. Cadence knew she couldn't take much more without wanting to regain control.

"Raven, sit behind her and remove her top."

Cadence wondered how far she'd have to take them before she could get her next clue. At the moment, she wanted to take them all the way, the thought of having to stop unsettling her. She was so close to orgasm herself she knew stopping would nearly kill her.

She kept going, too turned on to question anything further. She knew the others were as well. The tension in the room was palpable. The hot breath of the candles mingled with the hot breathing of the women. They were all turned on and breathing fire like it was desire escaping their bodies.

Raven slid in behind Ginger and unzipped her halter. She removed it with ease and tossed it aside. Then she sat with her hands on her thighs, awaiting instruction, her chest heaving and coated with sweat.

"Touch her breasts," Cadence said. "Slowly."

Raven ran her hands up Ginger's sides and began carefully touching her breasts. Ginger sighed and fell back against her. She laughed with delight and danced beneath her.

"Good," Cadence said.

"Now, Ginger, you stand. Stand with your back to Raven and allow her to remove your shorts."

Ginger stood and her gaze fell upon Cadence. She grinned wickedly and flicked her braid back behind her. Her muscular physique glowed in the firelight as every woman in the room was mesmerized by her form.

"Sit back down," Cadence said. "Between Raven's legs."

Ginger returned to the bed and nestled back into Raven. Both women focused on Cadence.

"Raven, kiss her neck." Cadence began to round the bed again. "Good, now lick her ear."

Ginger groaned, already aroused.

"Run your hands over her breasts, teasing her. Awaken her as if she were a flower about to bloom."

Raven did as instructed, and Ginger began to gyrate back into her with her eyes closed.

"Does it feel good, Ginger?" Cadence asked.

"Mmm. Yes."

"Is she awakening you?"

"Oh, God, yes."

"Raven, attack her neck again as you continue to play with her breasts. Pay careful attention to her nipples now. You want to get her nice and wet."

"Oh, God!" Ginger cried out as Raven complied. She cupped Raven's hands and undulated into her.

"Nuh-uh-uh," Cadence tsked. "Ginger, lower your hands. You have no control here."

Ginger dropped her hands but stammered. "But it—it feels so good."

"I know," Cadence said.

"I need more."

"I know."

"Hurry."

Cadence laughed and looked to the surrounding women. "What do you think? Should we give her more?"

Silence.

"I don't know, Ginger. No one is speaking up. Guess we'll just have to keep teasing you."

"No." She shook her head. "No, please. I need it. I—need it."

"What do you need, Ginger?"

"To be touched."

"Where?"

"Here." She placed her hand between her legs, but then quickly removed it.

Cadence laughed again. "It's okay, Ginger. You can leave your hand there. In fact, why don't you? Why don't you put your hand there and do what you want with it?"

Ginger hesitated but then did so. She grazed her hand up her thigh and rested it on her glistening flesh.

"Go on," Cadence said. "Touch yourself."

Raven groaned behind her and massaged her breasts and nibbled her neck. Ginger sank her fingers into her folds and began to stroke, moaning and falling back into her.

"Oh, Christ," Raven said, feasting on her delicate skin. "Let me do it. Please."

"You want to touch her?" Cadence asked.

"Oh, hell yes."

"You want to see how wet she is?"

"Yes, please."

Ginger moaned again as she threw her head back, lost in her own world of pleasure.

"Is that what you want, Ginger?"

"Ye-es."

"Are you sure?"

"Yes." Her hand circled with increased speed, and she began to pant as Raven gently tugged on her nipples.

"Then stop."

Both women froze.

Both panted as they waited.

"Ginger, lean back into Raven and spread your legs wider. That's it. Good. Actually, why don't you place your legs over hers? Good. Yes. Now, Raven, you may touch her. Touch her for all of us to see."

Raven started by kissing her ear, and then down to her neck. When she reached her shoulder, she began to graze her hand up her thigh and into her wet pussy. The seashell pink of her glistened in the firelight and Raven sank into her folds with obvious expertise, causing Ginger to throw her head back and sigh.

"How does she feel?" Cadence nearly choked, almost too moved by the sight before her to speak.

"So good," Raven said. "So fucking wet."

"Mmm. She's nice and slick, then?"

"Oh, fuck yeah."

"Then stroke her. Nice and slow. Like the most delicate and ornate of violins. One you've waited your whole life to play."

Raven did as instructed, taking Ginger slowly. She gently moved her hand on and around her pussy, careful with her fingers to play her engorged clit like the finest of instruments. Ginger gritted her teeth and moved her body like the finely tuned instrument it was, bringing herself into perfect synch with Raven. It was magical to watch, magical to witness.

And Cadence wasn't the only one fascinated. Around her, the women were as still as the night, but their bated breathing gave them away. And some began to make noises of their own. Small, meek noises of helplessness and some, deep, guttural sounds of desperation.

All while the erotic dance on the bed continued.

And that's when Cadence got an idea.

"Who wants her to come?" she asked.

Silence.

She asked again.

"Don't hold back now. Who wants to see her come?"

"Me."

"I do."

"I do, too."

Voices rang out, some meek, some strong. Cadence decided to go with a meek one.

"You. There." She pointed at one of the women. "How would you like to make her come?"

The woman just looked at her, obviously confused.

Cadence motioned for her to come forward.

"What's happening?" Raven asked from the bed.

"I'll make her come," the quiet woman surprised them all by saying.

"Good, come here then."

The woman came forward and Cadence spoke to her from behind while holding her shoulders.

"Go to her. Go to her and help Raven make her come."

She gently urged her forward and the woman moved to the edge of the bed and dropped to her knees.

Around them, the rest of the women began to hiss yes and encourage her.

"Raven, she's going to help you make her come."

"How?"

"She's going to suck on her clit while you stroke her."

"Fuck," someone whispered.

"Yes," someone else said.

"Hurry," Ginger let out. "I'm close."

"You heard her," Cadence said. "You had better hurry."

"Do you want to come with her, baby?" Raven asked.

"Yes."

"You want to come with her eating you out while I touch you and hold you?"

"God, yes."

"Okay, then."

Raven increased her speed and Ginger turned her head for a deep kiss, while the woman eased closer and began licking her thighs.

Ginger cried out and begged again for her to hurry.

"How does she taste?" Cadence asked.

"Like heaven," the woman said.

"Then take her," Cadence said. And the woman did. She kissed her way up Ginger's thigh and then fastened herself to her. Ginger shrieked with sweet mercy and knotted her hands in her hair and held her fast to her.

"Yes, yes, yes!" she cried. "Oh, God! Oh, Christ, yes!"

"Come, baby," Raven said.

"Yes, come now, Ginger. Come for all of us."

"You want me to come?" Ginger said as the woman's mouth smacked against her pussy and her toes curled at the edge of the bed.

"Yes!" The room nearly exploded in answer.

And Ginger came, exploding with her powerful orgasm.

She screamed like a woman coming apart and fucked the face of the woman between her legs while simultaneously kissing Raven as best she could, her body rocking all the while.

The women in the room made their own noises and Cadence watched with voyeuristic delight as Ginger came with one woman feasting on her between her legs and the other at her back, stroking her and holding her. It was a sight to behold, and she knew she'd never forget it. And she wanted desperately to share it with someone.

But as she looked around, she realized she still couldn't locate Emory and wondered just how long she could wait out this game before needing to reach her own climax.

Just then her own question was answered in part when another woman stepped forward and retrieved the next clue from the bed. She walked slowly up to Cadence and smiled as she handed it over.

"I believe this is for you," she said, as she opened the door and disappeared from the room.

Cadence swallowed against a dry throat and followed her, leaving the voyeur's delight behind to be consumed by the firelight.

Chapter Nine

The party was still in full swing as Cadence exited the bedroom and headed back into the main part of the house. The music thumped, women shrieked with laughter, and glasses clanked. She made her way back to the jellyfish bar and slid onto a stool. The bartender, the one who'd served her before, served her another rum and Coke.

"Looks like you could use it," she said with a smirk.

Cadence took the drink and gulped. Damn, she was thirsty.

"Thanks," she said as she set the glass down. "I guess I do."

"You been having fun?" the bartender asked, towel-drying a set of shot glasses.

"Mmm, what do you think?"

"I'd say by your red face and chest that yes indeed, you've been up to something fun."

"You'd be right."

The bartender noticed the red envelope and nodded toward it. "You gonna open that?"

Cadence glanced down at the red velvet rectangle. "Does everyone here know about this little game but me?"

The smirk appeared again. "Not everyone."

Cadence laughed. "I don't know why I'm surprised. Elizabeth loves to go all out with things."

"That she does."

"I just...I can't figure out how she knows Emory. I can't figure out how they got together to plan all this."

"Maybe you're not supposed to figure it out. Maybe you're just supposed to enjoy it."

Cadence finished her drink, still dangerously thirsty. The alcohol warmed her skin even more and softened the edges of her surroundings.

"Good point."

She fingered the envelope and readied herself for another adventure. Carefully, she opened the flap and pulled out the black card inside.

Dancing was fun.
Directing even better.
But now it's time to touch.
Come to the cabana behind the pool if you're game.

Cadence smiled as her heart rate kicked up once again. She held up the envelope and spoke to the bartender.

"Guess I'm off again." She slid from the stool. "Wish me luck."

"Oh, you don't need luck. Only your hands." She winked at her.

Cadence wanted to ask her if she somehow knew what the card said, if she knew anything, but something told her it would be pointless. Everyone seemed to be in on the game, and they were all very good at being cryptic.

Cadence turned from the bar and made her way out to the pool. The smell of chlorine lingered, and women splashed and played in the changing colors of the pool, all while keeping their masks on. Some hung around the edges making out, others sat at the in-pool bar talking, and others ran around the pool deck chasing each other. A good time was being had by all.

It made Cadence smile as she sidestepped an amorous couple giving chase. She found her cabana directly ahead, a ways behind the pool, a short distance from another, similar-looking cabana. The one she was headed for was closed, so no one could see inside, and she wondered, not for the first time, what she was about to step in to.

"Here goes nothing," she said as she stepped through the thick grass and pulled back the yellow striped material that hung at the doorway. Immediately, she noticed the scent of something spicy, and as she stepped inside, the noise from the pool seemed to fade away. The flap fell closed behind her and she had to wait a moment before her eyes adjusted in the dim light.

"Hello?" she said, as a few burning soft lamps came into view.

"Come in," a smooth voice said.

Cadence remained still, uncertain.

"Come on, I won't bite."

She took a step inside, and two women flanked her, one taking her envelope and the other leading her gently by the elbow.

Cadence fell into step and allowed herself to be led to a woman sitting on a stool. She was wearing a satin robe that shimmered a royal blue in the candlelight. Her mask matched her robe, and her mouth, which was beautifully shaped, seemed to match her melodious voice.

"Welcome," she said. She smiled and held out her hand. Cadence took it and the woman stood. She walked them to the back of the cabana where she offered Cadence a seat on a settee.

The woman eased onto another stool, this one elongated and thickly padded, and crossed her glorious legs.

"Tell me, have you ever had a massage?"

Cadence straightened. "Yes."

"Did you enjoy it?"

"Yes."

"Hmm. But did you really?"

Cadence cocked her head.

"Did you really enjoy it? You see, I find that the typical massage lacks real intimacy. Don't you agree?"

"Well, yes. Depending upon who's giving the massage."

"Precisely. So let's say that I want you to give me a massage."

"Okay."

"Uh-huh. Only I want you to…really enjoy giving me the massage. And I want to really enjoy you giving me the massage. Follow?"

"I think so."

"But first," she said, "I want you to watch. You don't mind watching, do you?"

Cadence couldn't help but heat from being pegged so easily. "I don't mind."

The woman smiled. "I didn't think so." She stood and untied the belt to her robe. The robe fell to the floor in a whoosh and one of the women rushed to scoop it up.

"My name is Camille," the woman said, watching her assistants with obvious amusement. She was completely nude save for a belly button chain that wrapped her abdomen like a delicate snake, and Cadence couldn't help but wonder what it looked like when her body moved.

"And this is Arie and Bailey. They're my helpers, so to speak." The two women nodded slightly toward Cadence and then continued moving at the other side of the cabana.

"I'm Cadence."

Camille laughed. "Yes, you are."

She continued to smile as she waved Arie and Bailey over. The two once again rushed over, this time carrying things in their hands. The light was dim, but Cadence could easily make out the white and pink swirled dildo Bailey carried. She handed it over to Camille and the two got busy placing the phallus in a leather strap. Then they busied themselves fastening the strap onto the elongated stool, so that the dildo sat pointing upward in the center of the cushion.

Cadence swallowed hard, imagining what was to come. She continued to watch as Arie lit two more small lamps, bringing the breath of added light into the room. Now, Cadence knew, she'd have a front row seat to something no doubt spectacular.

Camille stood before her like a goddess, all confidence and grace, and when she spoke, it was as if the entire party faded away beyond the cabana, leaving the four of them totally and completely alone.

"Now, the show begins," she said.

She nodded at Bailey and Arie and then locked eyes with Cadence as the two women then raised clear bottles above her and began pouring what appeared to be oil down her body. The luscious-looking liquid cascaded down her shoulders to her full breasts and below, to the snake-like body chain hanging at her torso. The sight was something to behold, the oil bringing her body to life in the lamplight, causing her to gasp in obvious delight.

"Do you like what you see?" Camille asked, breaking a grin.

"Yes," Cadence croaked. "Very much."

"Oh, but there's so much more," she said. She waved Bailey and Arie off and they stopped pouring and dropped the empty bottles to the ground. Then they took Camille by her hands and helped her onto the stool. Camille straddled it carefully and then watched as Bailey retrieved a tube and squeezed a clear gel-like substance onto her hands. Then she massaged the gel onto the dildo, bringing it to shimmering life as well.

"Perfect," Camille said. And with Bailey and Arie's help, she lifted herself and straddled the dildo, allowing the phallus to slide up inside her. She sighed and made a little squeal of pleasure as she sank onto it fully and swung her dangling legs.

"Oh, that's nice," she said, moving her body to and fro. "So very nice."

Cadence swallowed again, transfixed on Camille and her dance with the dildo.

"Tell me, Cadence," she said, still softly undulating on the phallus. "Do I look good enough to eat?"

Cadence pressed her lips together, praying her throat would open up to allow her to speak. "Yes."

"I was hoping you would say that." She smiled a wicked smile and Bailey and Arie came to her sides. "You see, the body oil is edible." Camille arched herself in an offering, and the two began to lick at the oil that was now beading on her body.

"Oh, yes," she hissed. "That's nice, girls. So very nice." She closed her eyes and feasted on their feast of her, using her hands to knot in their hair and hold fast to them. "Be sure to get it all, now," she said. She undulated quicker as the two women began to lick and suck at her body, careful to avoid her nipples or anywhere that the oil hadn't fully saturated.

"Good girls," she said with a laugh. "Such good girls." She danced a little more and then paused, opening her eyes to look down at her breasts and then at Cadence. "Oops, looks like they missed a spot or two."

She released her grip on the women and curled a finger at Cadence.

"This is where you come in, lovely lady," she said.

Cadence rose on shaky legs and walked to the stool. Camille leaned forward, almost touching her face nose to nose and spoke. "Touch me," she said. "Take your hands and rub this oil into me...everywhere."

Cadence blinked and breathed hard. "O-kay."

Camille took her hands. "Here, I'll show you." She rubbed Cadence's hands into the thick oil and helped her spread it all over her breasts and torso. "That's it. That's right. Now my girls can really dine."

Camille released her hands and Cadence started to back away, but Camille stopped her. "No, no. You have to stay." She grinned while Cadence took a small step back to watch. "The view is so much better from here."

Camille knotted her hands in Bailey's and Arie's hair and they began licking her again, this time fully attacking her nipples as she rocked into the dildo and stared into Cadence's eyes.

"Oh, yeah. Oh, such good girls. Oh, fuck yes. Lick me, ladies. Lick me real good." She called out and closed her eyes, the ecstasy obviously too much. "Fucking suck on my tits. Yeah, that's it. Oh, God yes."

Cadence burned at her commands and moisture pooled between her legs. She was tempted to press against the corner of the stool to garner some relief, but she held back, too impassioned to move.

Smacking sounds ensued as Bailey and Arie licked and sucked at Camille's breasts. They teased her hardened nipples with quick flicks of the tongue and then fully enveloped them with full tugs of the mouth, driving her nearly insane. She fucked the dildo fiercely, calling out, commanding, crying to the stars above, holding the women fast to her breasts as she did so.

"Fuck," she cried. "Oh, fuck yes. I love you, girls. Love you so much. I'm so close."

Cadence was right there with her, about to spill over herself at the slightest of touches. But that's when Camille stopped. She stilled on the stool and panted, massaging the women's hair as they came up for some much-needed air.

Camille kissed each one of them fiercely and then looked to Cadence.

"I want to come," she said. "I want to come now."

Carefully, she crawled off the dildo and watched in a daze-like state as Bailey and Arie moved the stool to the side and slid up a long, cushioned bench. Grabbing Camille's hands, they helped her onto it and eased her into a supine position. Then they each took a leg and gently opened her up, spreading her apart. Her pussy was dark pink and soaked, her thighs marked with her excitement. Her chest heaved as she lay back, her body still very much excited.

"Come touch me, Cadence," she said, lifting her head. "Come massage me while I come."

Cadence rounded the cushioned bench and walked to the head where she looked down upon Camille and began carefully rubbing her chest. Her skin was thick with oil and burning hot from pleasure.

"Mmm," Camille said, closing her eyes. "Now, help the girls out. They're going to pour more oil on me and you have to spread it around."

Bailey and Arie did as instructed and Cadence, with a racing heart, began massaging the oil into her. All over her breasts, her torso, and even down onto her thighs. Then they poured some between her legs and Camille nearly came up off the bench.

"Oh, God. Oh, fuck that feels good." She grinned up at Cadence. "Don't worry, Cadence. You don't have to touch me there. The girls know what to do."

And with that, Bailey and Arie began licking her again, this time working her entire body, causing her to call out and writhe.

Her commands soon became heated and heavy once again.

"Cadence," she called. "Massage me. Rub my tits while I come."

Cadence walked to the head of the bench and began massaging her full, slick breasts, while down below the women worked the rest of her body with their mouths.

"That's it," Camille said. "Fucking feast on me, girls. Yes, that's it. Now you know what to do."

The women moved up her legs to her center where they both began to flick at her pussy with their tongues.

Camille lifted her head, eyes wide open. "Yes," she shouted. "Oh, God, yes." She held fast to their heads while she thrashed back and forth.

"Fucking eat me. Eat me so good. Oh, God it's heaven. It's pure fucking heaven."

Cadence slowed her massage, lost in the sight before her. Bailey was attached to Camille's clit while Arie licked at her opening. Then they traded. Then they both focused on her clit once again. And as she screamed near orgasm, the women dove in further and sucked her all in as best as they both could, causing Camille to shriek like she was dying.

"Oh, my God! Oh, my fucking God, yes. Suck me. Suck me so fucking good. Make me feel so fucking good."

Her head thrashed and her hands flew up to Cadence's where she gripped her tight and rubbed her into her breasts. Cadence met her full force, giving to her until she fell quiet, and then stepped back a little as Camille released her. Bailey and Arie lay on her thighs, completely spent, mouths swollen and tinted red. Camille lay limp, chest heaving.

"That was some massage, Cadence," Camille eventually said. She laughed.

"I have to agree," Cadence said with a dry mouth.

"Bailey, get her the envelope. She earned it," Camille said.

Bailey stood and headed for the dresser near the front of the cabana. She returned with the red envelope and handed it over.

"Good-bye, Cadence," Camille said with glassy eyes. "It was nice to meet you."

"Likewise," Cadence said, wiping her hands with a towel and then taking her envelope and leaving. She stepped back out into the noisy night and stood very still. Glancing down at the envelope, she hoped that this would be the last clue. Because she couldn't take much more without wanting to take care of herself.

CHAPTER TEN

Cadence slipped off her heels and walked across the grass like a woman drunk on desire. She was so wound up, she was afraid she'd spill over at the slightest of touches, yet she was so heady, she thought she'd slur her words if spoken to. What a predicament to be in.

She laughed a little as she walked past the pool, careful not to stare too hard at the various couples making out, and headed back to the jellyfish bar. Her wet feet hit the cool marble floor and sent a nice chill along her spine. She swung onto the barstool and held up a finger at a new, different bartender. This one had long, dark hair and eyes that matched, piercing the night like ink being reflected by moonlight.

For a second, Cadence was breathless.

"Rum and Coke," Cadence said.

The bartender busied herself with a glass and then approached and slid it to her.

Cadence stared. "What's this?"

"Water with fresh mint."

"But I ordered a rum and Coke." Cadence stared into her abyss-like eyes.

My God she's beautiful. She's...could it be?

She focused on her lips and on her nose, desperate to find the answer she was seeking. But the woman's mask covered too much and she spoke up, ending her examination.

"Yes, but what you need is water. Drink up." She winked at her and walked away to help another customer.

"But wait, I..." The woman didn't turn, and Cadence slumped in her seat and focused instead on the mesmerizing dance of the jellyfish. She mindlessly sipped at her water and got lost in thoughts of Emory. Where was she? Who was she? She glanced around but saw no one who held her interest. In seconds her water glass was empty. She hadn't realized how thirsty she'd been.

How does everyone here seem to know what I need before I do?

She chewed on some ice while her mind went to what lay hidden in the envelope. Could it be her last clue? Or was there going to be a lot more to this game of cat and mouse?

She had to admit she'd thoroughly enjoyed what she'd been through so far, so maybe more clues wouldn't be so bad. But then again, she really wanted to see Emory, and her body was damn near demanding it.

Cadence finished the ice and looked for the bartender to ask for another. To her surprise, a full, frosty glass was already there next to her, waiting.

"How did she do that?" She searched for her, but the bartender was nowhere to be found.

Confused, Cadence sipped at the fresh water and fingered the envelope. Should she open it? Or should she rest a bit first?

The night had come on to her like a freight train with the appearance of the first clue, and it might be nice to rest some. But then again, the way her body was thrumming, she knew there'd be no breaks, whether she rested or not. She needed to be with Emory.

With careful hands, she opened the envelope, pulled out the black card, and read.

Still thirsty?
Come upstairs if you'd like another.

This one, like the last one, is on me.
Emory

Cadence glanced upward quickly and scanned the bar. Patrons sat and mingled, and another bartender, this one with short blond hair, was tending to them.

"Damn!" She'd missed Emory. "How could I have not known that was her?"

Part of you did know. You couldn't tear your eyes away from her.

After downing one last gulp, Cadence grabbed her card and headed for the staircase, shoes in hand. She felt a little like Cinderella as she ascended, wondering if she dropped a shoe if Emory would be intuitive enough to find her beyond the mansion walls.

"She won't have to find me. I'm going to make this very, very easy for her."

She reached the second-floor landing and searched right and then left. Both were relatively quiet and dimly lit. She chose to go right, to follow the beat of more music. Only this beat wasn't as strong or as powerful as the one downstairs. It was more… seductive. She came upon a room with open, double-wide doors. Inside, bits and pieces of clothing and people glowed in black light, moving along to the slow beat. Many of the bodies were nude, painted in iridescent paint, shimmering as eager hands explored them. Women kissed, danced, and held each other tightly. While others were fused together in sexual embrace, undulating to the music, giving to each other. This wasn't the room for wild dancing, for beginning foreplay. This was the room for the real thing.

Hands skimmed sweaty bodies, mouths sucked on mouths, hips gyrated to perfect rhythms. Groans came from against the walls where women danced to a different beat. The beat of sex. Of pleasure, of the ultimate release. Hands up dresses, up skirts, down pants. Moving to that different beat, the ones fed by the bigger one. And hands clawed at backs, at shoulders, bit into flesh. Mouths hung open, eyes clenched closed. Cadence searched the room, doubting that Emory was there, but then she froze as she caught sight of those eyes. They were reflecting the bright white of Emory's shirt and they were fiercely trained on Cadence.

"She's here," Cadence whispered in disbelief. "She's really here."

As if she could hear her, Emory pushed off from against the wall and moved toward her. Cadence held her breath in her throat and watched as she almost glided across the floor to her. She was so unbelievably sexy in her white button-down shirt and black leather suspenders. She looked powerful in a way that Cadence couldn't describe.

"Emory," Cadence said as she came to stand before her.

Emory reached up and brushed her cheek. "It's me."

"Oh, my God."

"Shh."

"But I—oh, my God, it's really you."

"It is."

"I—I've been waiting all night. Gone from room to room—"

"Shh. I know. I've been with you."

Cadence paused. "What?"

"I've been with you. In every room."

"Even the last one?"

She smiled. "There was a place for me to watch from outside the cabana."

"Oh." She felt herself flush, knowing she'd been watched.

"I loved it," she said, touching her face once again. "Every damn minute of it."

"You did?"

"It turned me on. *You* turned me on." She held a finger to her lips and grinned.

"You weren't upset? Jealous, you know? At least a little?"

"Envious maybe. At all the women that got to interact with you. But not jealous. No. Know why?"

Cadence shook her head.

"Because now I get to do all those things with you." She leaned in and whispered in her ear. "It's my turn."

Cadence gripped her arms as a fire swept through her. "Oh, Jesus, Em. I can't wait."

"You don't have to. We can start right now." She took her by the hand and led her to the middle of the floor. "Care to dance?" She faced Cadence and pulled her in tight for a heated, heavy kiss. Cadence realized that she hadn't even been close to being drunk on desire before, for nothing could've come close to the elixir that was Emory. She tasted of honey, pure and dark, direct from the source, leaving Cadence spinning, desperate for more.

As if sensing her thoughts, Emory pulled her tighter and held her firmly by the backside and deepened the thick, heavy-honeyed kiss. Cadence groaned in sheer pleasure and clung tighter to her as Emory slipped her slick tongue in her mouth to explore. Cadence welcomed her with her own and another sort of dance ensued as they moved on the dance floor.

"My God, you taste good," Emory said when she eventually drew away.

"Mmm," Cadence said, her eyes closed, still moved by the kiss. "You do, too."

"Do I taste like the bite of the finest, most prized whiskey?"

Cadence shook her head. "No, you taste like thick, dark honey."

"Oh." She smiled. "I guess I'll take that."

Cadence touched her lips. "I will too, if you don't mind." And she kissed her again, this time tugging at her mouth, letting her know just how hungry she was for her.

"Oh, wow," Emory said. "You want a lot more."

"You have no idea."

"You could always show me."

"What did you have in mind?"

Emory shifted her body and placed her firm thigh between Cadence's legs. Then she pulled her to her tightly and began to rub her leg into her center, grinding against her.

Cadence called out, the pressure almost too much. "Fuck. Emory."

"You okay?"

"I'm so close."

"Yeah?"

"Mm-hmm."

"Well, we can't have you wanting now, can we?" She lowered her hand and slid it beneath Cadence's short dress. She found her panties and pushed them aside. Cadence sighed and gripped her shoulders.

"Em," she whispered. "If you touch me I'll die."

"Don't worry," she whispered in return. "I'll bring you back to life." And she dipped her hand in and touched Cadence's excited flesh, causing her to come off the ground and onto her tiptoes.

"Emory!"

Emory merely laughed and nibbled at her neck. "It's okay," she said. "Just follow me. Follow me and the music."

And she moved against her once more, grinding her thigh against her hand as it slid along Cadence's center.

Cadence kept calling out, kept trying to tell her to stop. But she didn't want her to. Even if it did mean coming in this room in front of all these people. She just simply didn't care.

"Emory!"

"Yes, baby. Come."

"I'm so close. So close. Fuck."

"Come, Cadence. Come while I glide my fingers into your wet folds. Into your gloriously wet pussy." She rubbed her harder, faster. "Tell me. Is it all wet because of me?"

"Yes!"

"How so?"

"All—the clues. The rooms. The—women. Oh, God, Emory."

"It made you wet?"

"Oh, fuck yes."

She laughed. "Good. Now come, baby. Come in my arms and join me on the beginning of our journey."

She nibbled her neck again and Cadence went over. She exploded in the room of glowing, pulsating bodies, holding fast to Emory, who held her close and allowed her to shatter into a million pieces. She came so hard she actually held on to Emory's wrist and fucked her hand, saturating it with her throbbing pussy. She just simply could not get enough.

"Fuck," she let out, completely breathless as aftershocks shot through her. She held fast to her wrist, though, careful not to let it go. She wasn't quite done needing pressure from her hand.

"I've got you," Emory said, seemingly sensing her need. She pressed firmly against her and managed to get a few more kicks from her hips with the heel of her hand. Then she slipped her fingers up inside her and grinned.

Cadence nearly fell over. "Em! What are you doing?"

"Just testing the waters."

"For what?"

"You'll see." She carefully slid her hand out from between her legs and took her by the hand. Next to them another couple met and found orgasmic bliss as the party continued on around them.

Emory led the way from the room to the hallway where they turned right again and came to a large set of double doors.

"What's this?"

"This is a private area." She dug in her pocket for a key and turned the lock. A green light illuminated, and they stepped inside and closed the doors behind them.

"Does Elizabeth know we're here?"

"She's the one who suggested it."

Cadence shook her head in disbelief. "That woman. I'm going to give her an earful next time I see her."

"Yeah, well, it won't be tonight. She's, uh, indisposed as well."

"No kidding?"

Emory smiled.

"By the way, how did you do this? How do you even know Elizabeth?"

"All questions will be answered by the end of the evening."

"Seriously? You aren't going to tell me?"

"Let's just say you made the mistake of giving me Elizabeth's last name."

"I did, didn't I?"

"Uh-huh."

"Very resourceful."

"I am a detective, you know."

"Well, what's next? Let's see, we've already danced. Are you going to direct next?"

Emory glanced over at her as they came to a stop in front of another door.

"Jesus, you are, aren't you?"

"You'll have to wait and see."

CHAPTER ELEVEN

E mory. Oh, my God."

"The night is yours, Cade. All yours."

"Well, what about you?"

Emory opened the door and motioned her inside. "Trust me, I'm having just as much fun as you are."

Cadence felt a small pressure on her lower back as Emory escorted her in.

"Welcome to our own little haven," she said softly.

The room was smaller than the last and lit up in hues of blue. It took Cadence a moment to focus, but when she did, she saw a tall, leather-bound cross in the back of the room with two nearly nude women flanking it. They had on black masks and black shiny bottoms. Their nipples were covered in black tassels.

"What's all this?" Cadence asked with a nervous laugh.

"It's your fantasy."

"My…" She looked to the large bed covered in a dark blue velvet-looking duvet. Numerous overstuffed pillows tried to hide the headboard, while candles burned on the bedside tables, casting a warmer glow across the bed. And off to the side sat an elongated bench, one similar to the one she'd just seen in the cabana. She felt her skin heat, knowing exactly what it was for.

"You don't remember our phone conversation late one night? The one where you told me you wanted to be tied up and serviced in a room full of midnight blue?"

Cadence felt her mouth fall open. "Yeah, but, Em, this is—too much."

"It's real. Is that what's scaring you?"

"I'm not scared. Just—overwhelmed."

Emory smiled and led her farther inside. Behind them the door closed and the two women at the cross moved toward them. They took Cadence by the hands and led her to the cross.

"Em, I'm—shy."

"Shy? After all you've been through tonight?"

"I know. I—shit."

"What if I told you it would turn me on? Like seriously turn me on? And that nothing will happen to you that you don't want."

Cadence blinked. "Then I would say okay. I would say okay a million times over."

Emory kissed her, softly and languidly. "If at any time you want to stop, you just say so, okay?"

Cadence nodded. She closed her eyes and allowed herself to be in the moment. She wanted nothing more than to feel and experience Emory, everything else be damned.

"Undress her," Emory said.

Cadence opened her eyes.

Emory was looking directly at her. "It's my turn to direct now," she said. "Is that okay with you?"

"Absolutely."

The two women began to undress her and she stood very still, allowing them to do so. Then they led her to the cross and strapped her in by her wrists and ankles. Her heart rate kicked up as she stared at Emory, who looked more determined than ever.

"I've never been tied like this before," Cadence said.

Emory grinned. "I know. You told me."

"You planned this whole night by the things that I've told you, didn't you?"

"I did."

"No one has ever done anything like this before. Done anything for me before."

"That's a shame, Cade. You deserve the world, and I'm determined to show it to you, one moment at a time."

Emory dragged over a chair and sat in it, directly in front of the cross. She relaxed with her hands on her thighs, her legs slightly apart. She looked so damn sexy, so fucking fierce sitting there in charge in her outfit and mask, it made Cadence groan.

"Enjoying yourself already?" Emory asked.

"Mmm, enjoying you. You look exceptionally hot tonight."

Emory laughed softly. "I'm not the only one." She touched her chin as if contemplating. "Although I have to admit, seeing you nude is by far passing the impression that the little red dress left."

"I wore that just for you. You said you loved the color red."

"Seems I'm not the only one who's been paying attention."

Cadence smiled. "You're not."

"Get the feathers," Emory said, and the women retrieved two long blue feathers.

"Tease her," Emory said. "Everywhere but her erogenous zones."

The women stepped up to Cadence and ran the feathers along her body, tickling her skin, careful to avoid her breasts and pubic area.

Cadence sucked in a shaky breath, the sensation awakening and quickly overwhelming.

"How does that feel?" Emory asked.

"Good," Cadence managed. "It feels good."

"Is it arousing?"

"Oh, God yes."

"Especially because you're already so turned on?"

"Mm-hmm."

Cadence's body trembled as she struggled to speak. Gooseflesh erupted all over her and she found herself biting her lower lip in anticipation. She wanted, was dying for more pressure, all over her body.

"I love how turned on you are," Emory said. "I mean really

love it." She ran her hand beneath her nose from where she sat and then snuck her tongue out to taste her fingers. "So fucking good you are, Cade. So insanely fucking good."

Cadence shook at the sight and tugged at her restraints.

"Shit, Em. I—I'm dying here."

Emory tsked. "Hardly."

"No—I—am. I swear."

Emory eyed the two women. "Circle her breasts. Careful to avoid her nipples."

The women complied and Cadence jerked again, the sensation maddening.

"Please, Em."

But Emory just sat and watched, her dark eyes glinting in the blue light.

"You're fucking beautiful, Cade. You know that?"

"Then please, give it to me. Make me come."

"You want more?"

"Yes!"

Emory nodded. "Tease her nipples now."

The women touched the feathers to her painfully erect nipples, and Cadence called out and jerked wildly at her restraints. Spittle flew from her mouth as her heart thudded in her chest.

"Fuck! Em, come—on."

Emory leaned forward and rested her hands just above her knees, elbows out.

"What do you want?" she asked. "Tell me."

"More. I want more. Pl—ease."

"How? Be specific."

"I want to be licked. Sucked. My nipples. Please."

"That would be nice, wouldn't it?"

Emory leaned back to her original position. "Now her pussy," she said. "Tease her pussy."

The women complied and ran the feathers across her wet flesh. Cadence kicked and bucked to no avail. The restraints were too strong and her body too shaken, too weak with desire.

"Em," she cried. "Oh, God, Em."

"Does it feel good, baby?"

"It's torturous. Fucking maddening." She clenched her eyes as the women continued, vacillating between her breasts and vagina. She could feel sweat on her brow and on her chest. Her body continued to tremble, starved for more, starved for pressure and for climax.

"I—don't know how much more I can take."

"Then do something for me," Emory said.

"Anything." She opened her eyes.

"I want you to think about all the interactions you had tonight. Think about them and how they made you feel."

"Okay." She closed her eyes again and thought of each room, each and every woman. Arousal soaked her center, and with every slight touch of the feather, she bucked and groaned.

"Is it turning you on, baby?"

"Yes!"

"You sure?"

"Yes!"

"I want you to think about all those scenarios with one difference in mind."

"What's that?"

"I want you to imagine them with me being there with you. Just you and me, acting out each clue. Because that's what we're doing tonight, Cade. We're reenacting each clue. First the dance and now the directing."

"Oh, fuck, Em. It's so good. I wish you had been there."

"I was there, baby. But more importantly, I'm here now."

"Then come to me," Cadence said with a weakening voice. "Hurry."

Emory gave a nod to the two women, and they hurriedly left the room, closing the door behind them.

"Now we're all alone," Emory said. "All alone at last."

Cadence hung from the cross like a rag doll, desperate and trembling.

Emory stood and walked slowly to the cross.

"The girls got you good and turned on, didn't they?"

"Yes."

"But you noticed that I didn't let them touch you."

"No."

"That's because you're mine. You're mine now, Cade."

Cadence blinked back sweat. "Yes, I am," she said.

Emory groaned as she ran her hands down Cadence's slick body. "So beautiful. So, so beautiful."

"Em." Cadence bucked. "Hurry."

"Hurry, where? Here?" She leaned in and teased her nipples with her tongue.

"Oh, fuck! Oh, fuck, Em!"

"Mmm." She took a nipple in her mouth and fingered the other one, squeezing just enough to cause her to buck wildly again.

She laughed. "So sensitive."

"Ah," Cadence breathed. "You have no idea."

"I'd like to." Emory moved to the other breast and did the same thing. She groaned as Cadence reacted once again.

"Such beautiful breasts." She ran her hands over them, lightly skimming her rock-hard nipples. Then she dropped to her knees and ran her hands down her torso to her hips. "And now for the best part," she said, licking her thighs.

"Oh, Em, hurry."

"God, I've dreamt about this." She looked up at her. "Watch me, Cade. Watch as I taste you." And she once again snuck out her tongue, this time to lick and flick her clitoris.

Cadence thrashed madly, clenching her teeth. She tried to control herself, but she couldn't. The sensation was just too much. It was just too damn much.

"I'm gonna come!" The climax was coming on full force, uncontrollable. "Em!"

Emory responded by taking her in her mouth and sucking, ensuring the orgasm would not escape her.

Cadence screamed into the night and thrust her body forward

as hard and as far as she could and held it there, insisting Emory take it all, take it all in her mouth.

Then, when she could absolutely take no more, she relented and thrashed, the feel of Emory just too damn much to handle anymore. She jerked and cried out, desperate to get away, but Emory kept on, giving and giving, and groaning as she did so.

"Em!" Cadence managed with a hoarse voice. "God, Em, I can't. No more."

Emory carefully released her and delicately kissed her before she stood and kissed her softly on the mouth.

Cadence kissed her back as best she could, nearly too spent to do much more.

"Fuck," she breathed.

Emory chuckled. "Yeah, no kidding. You would think you had been waiting for that all night or something."

"Yeah, you would think."

Emory moved to the side and unbuckled her wrist. Then she did the same to the other and the ones on her ankles. Cadence fell into her arms and Emory held her for a long moment.

"We still have one more clue to reenact, don't we?" Cadence said.

Emory drew away and brushed some loose hair from her forehead.

"We do."

"Oh, God, I'm not sure I have the strength."

"You do, babe. Trust me, you do."

Emory backed away, lifted a finger telling her to wait, and walked to the elongated cushioned bench, and Cadence couldn't help but smile.

"Oh, boy," she said, remembering the massage tent.

"Oh boy is right. Only this time…"

"This time, what?"

"This time, I'm playing along too."

"Oh, really?"

"Uh-huh. So you better get over here and undress me."

"What about my last clue?"

"I just gave it to you."

"No envelope this time?"

"You want one?"

Cadence shrugged. "I guess not. You're the best prize of all."

"I had hoped so."

Cadence walked up to her and began unbuttoning her shirt. "You hoped correctly."

Cadence unbuckled her suspenders and then drew her open shirt down over her strong, smooth shoulders. "Talk about beautiful," she breathed. "You're stunning." She ran her hands over her taut chest and then teased her nipples through her bra.

Emory inhaled sharply and reached up to finger Cadence's mask.

"Is it okay if I take this off now? I want to see you. All of you."

Cadence nodded. "I want to see all of you, too."

Emory removed her mask and tossed it onto the bed. Then Cadence did the same to Emory's. Her hand shook as she took in all of her for the first time in person. "Jesus, you're incredible."

"So are you," Emory whispered. "So are you."

"I can't believe you're here. You're real and you're here."

"I'm real, baby. And I'm right here."

She took hold of Cadence's hands and brought them down to the button on her pants. "Undress me," she said. "So we can come together."

Cadence trembled at her soft command and unfastened her pants. Emory stepped out of them quickly, after kicking off her shoes and socks. Then she stood before her in her black panties and bra, breathing heavily, her arousal obvious.

"You're so strong," Cadence said, again running her hands over her shoulders and arms. "Like a sculpted masterpiece."

Emory caught her hands and kissed them. "Hurry, babe. I don't think I can wait much longer."

Cadence grinned. "I know the feeling." And deftly, she

lowered her bra straps and removed her bra. Then she fell to her knees and pulled down her panties. Emory stepped out of them and walked to a dresser, where she opened a drawer.

"Now for the fun part," she said, holding up several dildos for inspection. "What size and color do you want?"

"They're all new?" There were six or seven of them, all varying in size and color.

"Of course. I brought them in this evening." She tossed them on the bed and Cadence chose.

"The purple one."

"Ahh, small but adequate." She picked it up and secured it in a set of straps and then attached it to the elongated bench. Next she chose for herself, one that was slightly larger and pink and secured it as well, directly across from the other.

"Are you ready?" she asked as she picked up a bottle of oil.

"I am."

Emory smiled and poured the oil on both the dildos and stroked the shafts, ensuring they were adequately lubricated.

"Now," she said, straightening and holding out her hand. "Let's get you settled."

Cadence took her hand and swung her leg over the bench. Then she settled over the purple dildo and locked eyes with Emory as she slid down upon it.

"Oh! Mmm." She closed her eyes as it filled her up, nice and full and warm.

"My God, I wish I could capture that look," Emory said. Then she did the same, swinging her leg over and carefully bringing herself down upon the dildo. Her beautiful face crumpled as she took it all in and made noises similar to Cadence.

"I know what you mean," Cadence said, reaching out to touch her cheek.

Emory met her gaze and kissed her palm. She poured oil in it.

"Rub this on me." She poured some in her own hands and rubbed them together so she could do the same to Cadence.

"It's cold," Cadence said as Emory touched her.

"It'll warm up," Emory said. "Trust me on that."

They both giggled a little as they covered each other in oil. But soon, after Emory gave them both more oil, they were quiet and focused, intent on the job at hand.

Cadence began to undulate as she massaged the oil into Emory's skin, careful to avoid her breasts. Emory did the same to her, only she went further and began rubbing the hot oil over her nipples.

"Ah! Oh, God. Em, that feels so—nice."

"I bet it does." She rubbed harder, faster, then got herself more oil and traced her fingertips down Cadence's torso.

"Here, let me show you," Cadence said, massaging the oil onto Emory's breasts.

Emory hissed her approval and began moving her hips in a similar motion to Cadence and soon they were both rubbing and fucking, kissing each other between hurried gasps of breath.

"This is so good," Cadence said. "Too good. Oh my God, it's so good."

"Fuck yes it is," Emory said, clenching her eyes.

"Look at me," Cadence said. "I want to look into your eyes, Em."

Emory opened her eyes and Cadence saw the dilation, the pure unadulterated desire filling them.

Cadence held up her hands and Emory interlocked their fingers.

"Come with me?" Cadence asked as they continued to writhe and fuck.

Emory nodded. She closed her eyes again but opened them quickly and refocused on Cadence.

"Thank you for this," Cadence breathed as the orgasm loomed closer. "For tonight—for all you did for me."

"No, thank you," Emory let out. "For being you. I loved every second of it."

"You loved watching me?"

"Fuck yes."

Cadence laughed. "I'm loving watching you."

"Yeah?"

"Oh yeah."

"Then let's come together. Watch each other come."

"Okay."

They gripped each other's hands tighter and thrusted harder. Cadence could feel the firm dildo stroking her insides like a sword of fire. She stared down at Emory, watching her do the same to hers, her wet pussy swallowing up the phallus.

"You ready?" Emory asked, drawing her attention back up to her flashing eyes.

Cadence nodded, barely able to speak. "Yes."

"Then come," Emory said, voice hoarse. Her eyes rolled back in her head and she jerked, once then twice, and then exploded, body gyrating madly, voice calling out and then caving in.

The sight of her crumpling in ultimate pleasure sent Cadence right over and she bucked several times more and then exploded herself, screaming into the night, eyes and hands locked with Emory, taking in everything about her in that moment. Her eyes, her face, her mouth, her sounds. And of course her beautifully slick body as it undulated, taking in all the pleasure it could muster.

"Cadence," she tried to call out, again and again. "Oh, fuck, Cade."

"Em," Cadence managed. "I—I—oh God, Em. This is a dream. A dream come true."

Emory smiled as the last of the powerful orgasm surged through her. "It is, isn't it?"

Cadence jerked a few more times and then stilled. "Yes."

They sat in silence for a moment, both breathing heavily, hands still clenched together.

"You're a dream," Emory finally said. "Cadence."

Cadence blushed despite herself. Emory released her hands and reached up and touched her face.

"Blushing. Even now. After all this."

Cadence covered her hand with her own and kissed her palm. "Can't help it."

"It's adorable. You're adorable."

Cadence smiled. "And you're sexy as hell, woman."

Emory leaned forward and kissed her and then carefully crawled off the bench. She helped Cadence do the same and then helped her to the bed, where she encouraged her to lie down.

"What about you?" Cadence asked as Emory let go of her hand to return to the dresser.

"I'll be right there."

She opened a drawer and retrieved something. As she turned around Cadence saw that it was a red envelope. Just like the others she'd received throughout the night.

"I thought you said there wasn't one," Cadence said, propping herself up on an elbow.

"I may have fibbed a bit." She handed over the card and slid onto the bed next to her.

Cadence took the envelope and opened it.

She drew out the black card and read.

Now that the night is through
Will you...
Cadence
Do me the honor of giving me your heart
As I am giving you mine?
Right here. Right now.
Hoping for many more nights of Decadence?

Cadence covered her mouth with a trembling hand. She glanced up at Emory and got lost in the dark abyss of her eyes.

"Yes, of course," she whispered.

Emory grinned. "You mean it?"

"Em, I would love nothing more than to give you my heart."

Emory pulled her in for a long, hot, sweet kiss while Cadence continued to speak.

"And to experience many more nights of Decadence. With you."

REDEMPTION

Renee Roman

CHAPTER ONE

"Just stop already. I told you I'm not going." Deidre Talson crossed her arms, tapping her foot in annoyance. She wasn't interested in anonymous sex, and everyone who paid attention to the night-life scene knew that's all the so-called masquerade party on the hill was all about. In fact, she didn't want sex with anyone. That wasn't entirely true, but the one person she wanted sex with was no longer available, so what was the point in going? It would take a miracle to change her mind, and even then the chances were slim.

"Do you have any idea what I had to do to score an invitation?" Becca asked, making a pouty face as if she hadn't enjoyed whatever she'd done to earn it.

"No, and I don't want to." Dee turned away, unable to look her best friend in the eye knowing she'd see how much the breakup with Max had hurt. Still did. Not that she could blame Max. The woman she'd been with had an hourglass figure, long wavy hair that shone, and a gorgeous smile. All the things Dee didn't have. "Please don't use a guilt trip on me." Becca wrapped an arm around her shoulders, making her defenses lower.

"I won't, hon." She gave her a sideways hug. Becca let go long enough to clip the invitation on the front of the black refrigerator before returning, the look of a reprimanded child on her face. "Tell me you'll at least think about it?"

Between Becca and their mutual friend Jill, they'd been begging her to go for weeks. Dee pursed her lips and shook her head, then recrossed her arms. "Go away." It was half-hearted at best, but she really had heard enough. "Besides, I don't have a mask."

Becca squealed, clapping her hands like a high school cheerleader. "I knew you'd say that. I've got just the thing." She flew out the front door.

What the hell is she up to now? Curious, Dee went to look out the front window, but she didn't get far. Becca charged back in, a garment bag slung over one arm and a couple of cinch string bags hung from her fingers. That was a lot more than one thing.

"I knew you'd come up with some lame excuse not to go, so Jill and I did a little shopping." She hung the garment bag on the kitchen door and set the other bags on the table. A third one dangled from her wrist. The package was wider and longer than the others and she could only imagine what it held. Dee was already sorry she hadn't ignored Becca's call and the ensuing ring of the doorbell.

"This," Becca said dramatically as she opened one bag, "is going to catch someone's attention." She carefully withdrew a mask. But it wasn't just any mask. This one had black and red feathers flaring from the top and sides of the black face piece. A line of rhinestones outlined the mask, and the cutouts for the eyes were made to look as though expertly done white liner had been applied along with tiny, glittering stones to dramatize the overall effect. It worked.

"Where did you find that?" Dee hadn't planned on asking. She didn't want anything to do with attending the Decadence Masquerade Ball, but she had to admit the mystique about no one knowing who was behind the mask did hold a certain appeal. She could be sad and disheartened without anyone seeing her pain.

"Does it matter?" Becca handed over the mask. "Besides, I had to find something to go with this." Becca unzipped the bag and freed the garment. The floor-length dress was the same dark red as the feathers on the mask, and a starburst of black sequins over one sleeveless shoulder was a dramatic effect that was spectacular, especially since there wasn't any shoulder material on the other side. The slits that ran up both sides went ridiculously high. "Isn't it exquisite?"

It was something for sure, but not anything she'd be able to pull off. "For a model maybe."

"You'll rock the fuck out of it. Trust me. I know these things. You own a spa, for goodness' sake. I'd commit a crime to have your shape." She pursed her lips into a half-smile, half-sneer. Whatever was coming next ought to be a dooz.

Becca handed her another bag. "You're going to need these."

The bag contained two pieces. Scraps of material that she'd hardly call underwear. There was barely enough silk, aside from two narrow bands that were nothing more than strings, to cover the smallest woman's crotch, and she wasn't small. "What the hell are these?" She let the barely-there undies dangle from her fingertips.

"Well, you certainly can't wear regular panties with that dress. Those should come right above your hip," Becca said in her no-nonsense way as she held them against her narrow waistline. "But the bra is a real piece of fashion." Becca snagged another bag and pulled out a larger piece of matching lace material and handed it to her.

The half-cup, strapless number *was* sexy, but all she could imagine was whether it would even stay in place, and how. "You expect me to wear that?" Her breasts were on the larger size, and she couldn't see how she'd be able to keep them from flopping out if she bent over.

"Look," Becca said as she moved her hand from her hip to snatch the bra, impatience written all over her face. "It's got straps. They just happen to be clear." She crooked a finger and snagged the loops before tossing it aside.

"Some women can get away with wearing that little number, but I can't compare to them. Not even close." Why couldn't anyone see she was just another plain Jane.

"You don't have to wear anything at all except for your mask. It's a sex party, you know. After a drink or two, you might be tossing all your clothes aside."

She made a face, one she'd used over the span of their friendship when something Becca was suggesting was more than a bit over-the-top, which was the case most of the time. "I've heard what goes on there and I have no intention of strutting around naked." She didn't. Wouldn't even consider it. Who would want her anyway? Max didn't. That was one thing she didn't have to guess about. Though the idea of seeing others in all their glory did pique her curiosity, even if she wasn't that proud of her own body. "Don't make me sound like a prude."

"Honey, the last thing you are is a prude." Becca held the mask up in front of her own face. "Want to find out what's beneath?" she said with a growl. She pulled the mask away. "What do you say?"

"Look, I appreciate the vote of confidence, but I really can't." Not that it wasn't tempting, but Dee imagined the night was supposed to be carefree and fun, and she wasn't in the mood for pretending to be interested in either.

Becca gently placed her hands on her shoulders. "But you should," she said, her voice gentle. "I'm leaving everything here in hopes you'll change your mind. It's an all-night party, so it's never too late to go." She kissed her cheek and squeezed her shoulders before leaving.

The invitation glared at her like a neon sign, telling her to get her shit together. Dee glanced at the mask, the gorgeous gown, and the embarrassingly miniscule undergarments. *Hell, I may as well not even bother with them, for all they cover.* Not that she was considering going. Of course not. She wasn't ready to have any sort of fun. No. No fun for her.

❖

Max paced her bedroom from one end to the other. *This has got to work.* She'd been frantic since the night Dee had walked out three months ago, believing Max was flirting with the actress she'd hired to make a new television commercial for her Alfa Romeo dealership when what she was really doing was putting Lisa at ease during the rehearsal. Not that the business was faltering. This was Las Vegas, after all, and there was no shortage of high rollers who wanted to show off their good fortune in style. She wasn't a millionaire, but she didn't want for anything…except for Dee.

Her heart ached in a way she couldn't describe. The love of her life was gone and the life she was walking through now was a hollow shell compared to what it had been with Dee in it. No more waking up beside the warmth of her. No more reaching between her long, shapely legs to find her wet and ready, even in sleep. Max loved that about her, too. How damn sexy she was, even if Dee didn't think so.

Becca and Jill had told her as much. That Dee believed it was the reason Max had turned to the admittedly gorgeous woman she had seen her with. But when she tried to explain what was going on, Dee waved her off and drove away with tears streaking her face and pain in her eyes.

As she fixed her bowtie, Max could barely breathe. How had she let Dee slip away? Maybe she should have begged to let her explain what she'd been doing with Lisa. Max stared in the mirror. Her face told the story of how much she missed Dee. Her features were drawn into a grimace and the shadows beneath her eyes were evidence of how little she was sleeping. Most nights she tossed and turned, reaching for Dee only to find the space beside her cold and empty.

Elizabeth Hathaway, a close friend and customer, had been

gracious in giving her two invitations after she'd explained about the misunderstanding with Dee and how she would do anything to get her back. Max had met Elizabeth shortly after she'd opened her dealership located just off the Strip. Elizabeth had wanted a candy apple red Alfa, and Max had made it happen. They'd struck up a friendship that very first day, and Elizabeth assured her she would do whatever she could to help Max win back her lover.

"I'm all about romance, with a healthy dose of hot, steamy, kinky sex." Elizabeth had handed her the invitations with a wink. "And to spice things up a bit, here's a raffle ticket. Use it in whatever way you can think of to have an advantage, just let me in on it so I make sure every part of the plan is ready." She placed her hand on Max's arm and gave a gentle squeeze. "It's going to be fine, Max."

She'd been more than a little surprised by Elizabeth's generosity. She had been sending Max an invitation for the last four or five years, but Dee hadn't wanted to join in the adventure, saying she had no interest in watching people have sex. Max wasn't one to put her nose up at any act that gave consenting adults pleasure, and she had the feeling if Dee would just go and give it a chance, her opinion might change. Either way, Max didn't care how much she had to rely on Elizabeth and her friends as long as the love of her life came back to her. She wasn't going to beg because she'd done nothing wrong, but she *did* want the chance to explain what Dee had seen wasn't in the least sexual. Lisa was a happily married straight woman who happened to be beautiful, too. As beautiful as Lisa was, she couldn't compare to Dee's lush curves, mesmerizing eyes, and infectious laugh.

Max sighed. All she could do was hope that her plan worked, because if it didn't she had no clue what she would do. What she *did* know was that giving up wasn't an option, and never would be.

CHAPTER TWO

Dee was fashionably late by the time she got in her car. She used the excuse of not wanting to have to try to blend into a nonexistent crowd when in reality she'd put the gown on no less than three times. All due to a conversation she had out loud with the mirror, going from she couldn't possibly wear this to what the hell did she care? No one would know her. The GPS's strident voice startled her into paying attention.

"Turn right onto the next driveway and follow the fork on your left."

She flicked on her high beams until she came to the gate, then slipped on her mask, ignoring the tremors in her hands. When she stopped, she held up the invitation with the QR code to the camera, as instructed. While she waited she considered turning around, but as the gate swung open, Dee somehow found the nerve to drive through. The driveway lit up as she approached and she couldn't help thinking how far out of her league Elizabeth Hathaway was, and for the hundredth time wondered what she was doing thinking she had nothing to lose.

The massive stucco mansion rose from the stone steps and ornate topiaries, making her feel small and inconsequential, the same way she felt most days lately. The variety of flowers and bushes that flanked the stone steps was no small feat, considering they were in the desert, but then someone as wealthy as E.H., as the invitation stated as the host, could afford it. Dee recognized honeysuckle and coneflowers among the blooming cacti.

A valet opened the driver-side door, introduced herself as Ruby, and greeted her with a warm smile and a slight bow. She was a red-lipped, well-endowed woman in a tux that left little to the imagination with her nipples acting as buttons on her tuxedo shirt. Dee grabbed her phone, then took Ruby's offered hand. Once she was standing on the driveway, Ruby waved to another masked woman who got in and whisked her beloved car off in the direction of a large grassy knoll where dozens of other expensive cars were lined up.

"Your vehicle will be available whenever you wish to leave," Ruby said. "Phones are not allowed inside. Please proceed to the tent where you can lock it up along with any other valuables for safekeeping."

She didn't like the idea of being cut off from the only way to contact what felt like the outside world. "What about tips?"

The woman's deep red lips moved into a generous smile. "We're all well compensated for what we do. There's no need to worry about anything except having a great time."

Dee nodded, unsure about what she was about to walk into. She never would have imagined being here, nor had she ever imagined being at a party like this without Max at her side. She let out a long breath, determined to at least make it through a drink, two at the most before she made her escape. Sooner or later, she'd have to drive home. Alone.

"Good evening," the tuxedoed attendant said from the entrance to the tent. "I'm Lisa." She opened a small locker. "Please place your valuables inside."

Reluctantly, she slid her beloved phone, along with her ID and credit card, into a metal box. Dozens of similar ones lined the space, many of which were missing keys. "How will I get it back?" Lisa locked the miniature locker, removed the key, and pointed to a small stand that held a laptop.

"With your permission, I'll take your picture and assign

a number to the file that will correspond to the number of the locker. Then, when you're ready, you can tell me the number and I'll verify your identity," Lisa said. She must have looked as hesitant as she felt. "The tent is always staffed. You won't have to worry about setting your phone down and losing it, and unless you have a hidden pocket I'll keep your key safely locked away." Lisa looked her up and down, making her face warm at the open appraisal. Lust. That's what she saw under it all. She didn't want to be there among a group of strangers who were also sexual deviants. The more she thought about it, though, the idea of being anonymous didn't sound so bad. Maybe she shouldn't be so quick to judge. After all, wasn't that the reason she was here alone?

"I'll leave it with you." After hearing her number, she looked at the mansion's grand entrance, her mind flip-flopping between why she was there when all she could think about was how much she was missing Max and, as Becca so eloquently stated, the prospect of getting laid without the usual "getting to know you" formalities. Maybe that was reason enough.

"Wonderful. Go right up the front steps. I think Shelly is just inside and can show you around. The jellyfish bar is on your right, but feel free to explore. The entire first floor and grounds are open to all guests. Enjoy." Lisa shared a heart-stopping smile below her Zorro mask before greeting another partygoer.

The steps were wide with a comfortable depth, the stone railing warm under her hand. She paused at the huge double doors, opened wide and welcoming. She could do this. If she did nothing else, she had to prove to herself that life as she'd known it was over and the future lay ahead. The idea of playing it safe hadn't worked out as well as she'd always believed it would, and the time had come to have new experiences. The second she crossed the threshold, she let out a breath. Just as the invitation stated, everyone around her was wearing a mask of one fashion or another. Some guests wore half-masks that didn't cover their mouth or chin, and like her, many seemed to gravitate toward the feathered Mardi Gras style. The sensual music that played in the background seemed to be coming from everywhere. The primal, alluring beat made her wish she wasn't alone.

"Excuse me. Do you need help?"

Dee turned to find a woman who wore an ornate half-mask and a shimmery, see-through floor-length dress that showed off her body more than covered it. She inhaled sharply when she saw the thatch of dark hair that was prominent between the woman's thighs, and she quickly averted her gaze. The woman's hand on her arm let her know her staring wasn't unwelcome. "I was looking for the bar."

The woman's hand fell away and she pointed. "The one through there is the nearest one. It's named the jellyfish bar, but I just call it the tank bar."

"The nearest? How many are there?" She could really use a drink, the sooner the better.

The woman's head tipped to one side. "Let's see," she began. "There's one in the pool, another in the theater, one in a tent outside, and one in the playroom." She laughed. "Of course, I might have missed one or two." She smiled. "I'm heading that way. Come on, I'll introduce you to the bartender. She makes a mean cocktail, and I'd tip her very well if it was allowed." She slipped her arm through Dee's as though it were the most natural thing in the world.

It took a few seconds for her vision to adjust to the muted lighting in the bar to be able to see the other guests, though the shimmering jellyfish in a huge wall-length tank were easy enough to make out at first glance. They took on the colors of the lights that shone up from the gravel bottom, and their languid movements and delicate tendrils floated in a mesmerizing dance.

"Beautiful, aren't they?" Her new friend tipped her chin and gazed at the tank.

"I've never seen so many in one place." The tank was filled with dozens of transparent creatures and, the glass was crystal clear, bringing everything inside in stark relief. Like a 3D movie that zoomed in and out. While she stood fascinated, another woman approached, bringing her out of her temporary daze.

"There you are. I wasn't sure you were going to make it." This woman wore a sleek black sequined drop-back, sleeveless dress that showed off her muscular arms and thick calves. The mask was in the Day of the Dead style of black and white. She was stunning. "There's someone I want you to meet."

"Have a great time and make sure you enjoy the scenery." The friendly woman smiled, and her tongue darted out to swipe at her lips. Dee had a feeling she was talking about much more than the mansion's décor.

"You, too." As lame as it sounded, she wasn't sure what else to say. The entrance behind her would provide an escape, but since she was there, she may as well have a drink. She moved among the growing number of bodies, some in full costume, while others wore little to nothing except for their mask, and Dee fought the urge to do more ogling. Her puritan-minded parents would have been proud she was resisting temptation even though they'd be mortified if they knew she was there. The bartender made eye contact as she reached the bar rail.

"Good evening, I'm Tosh," she said. "What can I get you?"

Had it been that long since she'd done something other than open a bottle of wine and wallow in self-pity? That kind of attitude had to be rectified. Dee blinked hard. Huh. Maybe doing something out of the ordinary was *exactly* what she needed. "Why don't you surprise me." Tosh was tall and lean. Her eyes shimmered with just the right amount of sex appeal and the lop-sided grin that appeared made her tingle in all the right places. She was just about to ask what she'd decided to make when Tosh began to unbutton her vest, revealing a tantalizing view of her high, firm breasts before she slid her hands inside and played with her nipples until the prominent knots poked at the fabric. Her face heated when Tosh leaned closer, and her mouth watered at the thought of sucking each one in turn.

"Was that an okay surprise?" Her silky voice had deepened.

"Oh yeah, that was more than okay." What the hell was she doing? She didn't flirt with strangers. Ever. If Max… "But I'm still thirsty."

Tosh stood tall. "I've got what you need." She moved to the shelves of liquor bottles that rose to meet the bottom edge of the tank. Snatch, pour, return. Three different spirits went into the shaker, along with a splash of something deep pink and then a drop of bitters. It was the one bottle that hadn't been moved in the blink of an eye, and easily recognizable by its shape. Tosh filled a tall, slender glass with ice, added some more ice to the shaker, then vigorously mixed. Her breasts didn't giggle as she shook it, but her nipples grew substantially, like diamond points against the confines of her vest. She tapped the top to separate it from the shaker cup, poured the concoction into the glass, added a slice of lime and a long, thin straw, and delivered it to Dee with an outrageously bright smile. "I hope you like it."

The glass looked delicate, and she carefully maneuvered the straw to her mouth, not wanting to hit the mask. Thank the gods she'd practiced drinking a couple of times before leaving the apartment, otherwise she might have ended up with the straw up her nose. The flavor that greeted her tastebuds was smooth, with just the right combination of tangy and sweet. Underneath it all was the alcohol, subtle but substantial. She'd need to nurse the cocktail if she wanted to hang around for a while. "It's really good," she said. "What do you call it?"

"A woman's blush." Tosh's eyebrow rose.

Apropos, considering the color of the mixture, and her face warmed at the intensity of Tosh's gaze. Dee reached for her absent cell phone. "I'm afraid I don't have anything on me to leave you a tip."

With a tilt of her head, Tosh grinned. "First time to the Decadence?"

"Yes." *First time being alone at any event without Max.* She kept that to herself.

"The whole point of tonight is not thinking about the

constructs of societal expectations. Tips aren't necessary. Doing what you want, with the consent of the other person or people, is all that matters. Relax and enjoy yourself."

What a novel concept. "Thank you, Tosh. I'm sure I'll be back for another of these." She turned to continue her exploration, slowly taking in the groups scattered around the space. People were friendly, smiling, touching, laughing. Some women were partially naked, but everyone appeared at ease, assuring her this was not like any party she'd ever attended.

Soft laughter and the murmur of conversation drew her attention, and she sucked in a breath. A woman with unruly dark hair and wearing a tuxedo moved at the edge of the crowd, and for a moment she could have sworn it was Max just by the way she carried herself, but that was crazy. There were a lot of women wearing tuxedos, and a number of them had similar physiques. She was the ugly duckling of the bunch, but lucky for her no one could tell, and once again she was grateful for the disguise. Wishful thinking on her part wouldn't pull Max away from whatever sexy woman she was with. She doubted anything could. Dee had severed that tie, and now it was too late to think a reconciliation was possible. The times she'd berated herself for acting rashly were only outnumbered by the times she cursed trusting Max with her heart. That didn't change the fact she missed her every minute she thought about her…and she constantly thought about her, wondering where she was and what she was doing. Dee shook off the melancholy. She'd come to have fun, something she was determined to find.

She followed a slow-moving stream of people to a large lounge that held an array of sofas and chairs, each one distinctly beautiful and made of soft-looking leather. Others mingled along the perimeter, content to watch women engaged in the conversations she overheard. They varied between light and jovial, to sexually explicit pleas of "I need to come. Let's fuck." Or an occasional declaration of "My clit's throbbing." Last year, Max had offhandedly mentioned the fifth-year anniversary of

Decadence, and she'd again brushed her off, saying she had no interest in "the porn fest goings on at *that* kind of a party." She hadn't wanted Max to think public debauchery interested her, or that she would ever attend an event that lacked decorum. In reality, though, she *was* interested. Everyone appeared to be relaxed and she had yet to hear a judgmental opinion. What would that feel like? To just do whatever she wanted without shame or guilt?

Honestly, she wouldn't mind mixing it up in the bedroom. Her upbringing and her mother's stern tone had haunted her into her early twenties, but she was just as curious about what other people did for fun as the next person. Well...all the people here anyway. Now that she thought about it, Max hadn't asked her to attend this year. Did that mean she'd given up, or that she'd already found someone to go with her? That sobering thought didn't sit well at all. After seeing what was happening around her, perhaps she'd come off more like a sex snob rather than not wanting Max to think she had an interest in the kinky side of consensual sex. But it wasn't true. In the right frame of mind... the right mood...she'd volunteer for a lesson. How was Max to know if she never told her?

Dee packed those surprising and random thoughts away and sipped her cocktail as she casually moved on to the next room and entered a semidark theater. The floor-to-ceiling screen was flanked by red velvet drapes. Sconces on opposite walls cast dim, intimate lighting, but she didn't have any trouble seeing. The screen displayed two naked women, one riding a large strap-on while the wearer played with her nipples. Moans filled the space. Some came from the movie; others were from women in the double-wide seats who were active participants acting out their own scenes. She stood staring at the grinding couples, all still wearing masks that added to the erotic nature of the atmosphere.

"Hot, isn't it?" An older woman with gray hair and a black half-mask stood next to her. She wore a black suit, gray shirt, and bright red lipstick, the only standout detail of her ensemble.

"They certainly are." She took a big gulp of her drink, nearly emptying the contents.

"I see Tosh made you one of her specialties."

"Mmm...hmm. It's very good."

The woman stuck out her hand. "I don't believe we've met. I'm Elizabeth Hathaway."

Her jaw nearly hit the floor. All these years, she'd had the notion that the host of what was rumored to be a decadent affair was a woman well into adulthood. "I'm Deidre Talson. It's nice to meet you. Ma—" Dee sucked in a breath. She didn't want Elizabeth to know she knew Max. They'd never met in person, and now there wasn't a need. "A masquerade party is such a wonderful idea." She finished her drink and wished she had about a gallon more.

"Thank you." Elizabeth looked around. "Are you here with anyone?"

She swallowed her pride and settled on the truth. "No. I wasn't going to come without a date, but my friends told me to make the most of it."

"Your friends are right, Deidre. Why don't we get you another drink? I'd like to show you something special." Elizabeth took her arm and guided her effortlessly toward the bar with the tank, her shoes clicking on the tiles in the foyer as they walked. "Have you been here long? Is this your first time?"

The questions were casually asked, making her feel at ease to answer. "Yes, first time, and I'm not really sure how long I've been here." Wasn't it odd that she had no concept of time since she'd arrived? She held up her empty glass. "One drink in." She kept her tone light, but it was a facade, just like the masks that hid everyone's identities.

Elizabeth chuckled. "About an hour, then. Not nearly enough time to take it all in." She stepped up to the bar and Tosh appeared. "And you simply must see it all." Elizabeth turned to Tosh. "Two of whatever you gave my new friend, Deidre."

"Humph. Deidre, eh?"

"You mean to tell me you didn't find out this gorgeous woman's name right away? You must be losing your touch, Tosh." Tosh's face fell. "Now, Tosh, you know I'm teasing. I rather forced her into telling me. Didn't I, dear?" Elizabeth turned so that Tosh couldn't see her wink.

Oh, this was fun. "It's true. Elizabeth practically cornered me. What could I do?"

"Yeah, she's pretty hard to resist." Tosh set two tall glasses down and winked. What was it with all the winking? Tosh proceeded to make more of the magical drink that had settled into a nice buzz.

"Maybe I shouldn't have another one. I have to drive home at some point."

"Nonsense. I have drivers for whoever needs transportation home, so that's not an excuse to not have fun." Elizabeth handed her a glass then sipped from the other. "Excellent as always, Tosh. Stop by my office tomorrow. You deserve a bonus."

Tosh's facial expression remained a mystery, but her words conveyed everything. "Your generosity is appreciated, Elizabeth."

Dee waited for the wink that never came. Okay, so the winking wasn't a constant thing. Maybe it was an inside joke between them.

"Shall we?" Elizabeth pointed to the open French doors.

Considering the temperature of the bar, the minute she stepped outside, the heat greeted her. It wasn't the same intensity as daytime, and being up on the top of a hill likely helped keep it tolerable. The mask only added to the warmth, and she could feel moisture forming on her upper lip.

"Are you warm, dear?" Despite her formal wear, Elizabeth appeared comfortable. As they descended the stone steps toward the pool, a cool breeze swirled around her, and she soaked in a moment of relief.

"A little. I spend so much time in air conditioning, I don't think I've ever properly acclimated." She took a refreshing sip and looked to where Elizabeth pointed.

"I've had cooling fans installed throughout the property for occasions like this. I'd prefer if my guests didn't melt." Elizabeth smiled and continued to lead her around the large pool. Off to one side was a floating bar. The two bartenders were naked except for the requisite masks they wore. Their bodies were thicker, like Romanesque statues, but nonetheless beautifully curvy. Elizabeth must have caught her looking in their direction. "I believe the world needs to show its appreciation for women of every shape and size. My staff are representative of that belief."

Dee had to admit, she'd not really given much thought to the sentiment, but as she took a more focused look around, she saw women of all shapes and sizes, clothed and naked, who appeared comfortable in their bodies, so unlike Dee's view of her own. This was a woman's paradise to be sure. "I couldn't agree more," she said, wishing she were half as confident in her willowy shape.

"What type of woman are you attracted to, Dee?"

Tears welled and her vision swam. Max had always been the perfect woman in her eyes. "Tall. Strong. Handsome. But their character must be paramount. Kind, caring, open, and honest." How could she describe her ex-lover in a way that would encompass all of Max's most endearing traits? Dee's heart sank. Max hadn't told her she wasn't happy in their relationship. That hurt most of all.

"Why don't you go inside and relax a bit. I'll send someone to take care of you." Elizabeth held the curtain of a cabana aside. It was one in a long row of similar tents, spaced out on the grass just behind the pool. A soft breeze from a small fan in the corner kept the air moving, and the padded lounge chair with a mass of pillows looked inviting.

She couldn't think about anything other than how much she missed Max. How she craved her in every possible way. She was tired of the ongoing battle between her heart and her head.

Dee had listened to her head, but her heart refused to cooperate. She hadn't even noticed that Elizabeth had slipped away while she had the internal conversation, so she gave in and spread out on the surprisingly comfortable chair. Of course, from every appearance, Elizabeth spared no expense. Naturally, it would be the same outside as it was on the interior. She certainly knew how to throw a party. Dee took another swallow, then set down her cocktail, letting the mellow music wafting from every direction soothe her. Her eyes grew heavy and slowly closed. *Just a few minutes, that's all I need.* If she thought about it, it would take forever to come to terms with losing Max to someone who was younger and stunning in every way. She wished she was describing herself and had what Max wanted, but it was obvious she didn't.

CHAPTER THREE

"S he's in the third cabana, but I'm not sure how long she'll stay put," Elizabeth said.

"Do you think she'll recognize me?" Max's painted-on tuxedo and matching painted mask had been done in such a way as to disguise her true features. She'd checked herself out in a full-length mirror. The results were startling enough she didn't recognize herself, but Dee intimately knew her and every detail of her body. At least, she hoped so, except for tonight. Tonight, she wanted to be whomever Dee needed, or wanted.

Elizabeth lightly put her hand on Max's arm. "Max, I barely recognized you. If we hadn't prearranged a meeting spot, I would have never known it was you."

Her hands were sweaty. The artists who worked on her had assured her she'd have to use the special soap they'd delivered to her room in the mansion when they'd brought up her discarded tux. The last thing she wanted to worry about was revealing herself before the time was right. She needed to get moving before she started questioning her plan. "Okay. I'm going." She reached for Elizabeth's hand. "Thank you for everything."

"Don't thank me yet. You're the one who must do the work." Elizabeth gave her a squeeze. "Dee would be a fool not to want to reconcile. If you need anything, you know how to find me."

Max nodded and turned toward her destiny. The cabanas were mostly unoccupied, but that would change as the night wore on. She'd come to the first masquerade party solo, when she and Dee were dating, prior to their living together. It had been an education into a world where there was no judgment when it came to consenting adults and their ability to express themselves sexually or otherwise.

She pulled back the curtain and smiled though her heart ached. Dee reclined on the lounge with her eyes closed. She wore a beautiful red dress and a matching fully adorned and feathered mask, but she'd know her anywhere. The small lamp in the corner cast enough light that if she announced herself, Dee would be able to see her. Well, hopefully, she'd see *someone* without recognizing it was her. Fingers crossed.

"Good evening," she said, keeping her voice deeper than usual. Dee's eyes opened behind the mask. "The host asked me to take care of you." She moved closer. "May I?" *Please say yes.* She waited, fighting the urge to beg out loud.

"Who are you?"

She'd thought long and hard about what her answer would be if Dee asked. "Redemption."

Dee stared at her, her chest moving up and down rapidly. "Yes, you can." Dee whispered so low she could just make out the words above the background noise. "I need it."

Max couldn't be sure if Dee was giving her permission to touch her or not, or if she was simply agreeing to be taken care of in a way only Dee knew. This wasn't the time to nitpick. She bent over her, gathered the fabric of her dress, and slid it up until it pooled at her hips, revealing a miniscule black thong. Had Dee ever worn such tantalizing garments when they were together? Max was certain she'd remember if Dee had, and it was all she could do not to moan. Dee was firm about her position when it came to kinky sex, or anything that was the least bit erotic, which had struck her as the antithesis of how she saw Dee. From the first moment she'd seen her from across the room, Max thought she was one of the sexiest women she'd ever met, though according to their friends, Dee never believed it.

She lay on the chaise lounge on her stomach, her face inches from Dee's crotch. Dee inhaled sharply. Their eyes met as she pulled the thong to the side. Max only waited a beat, afraid if she hesitated Dee would change her mind, and used her tongue to stroke the silky layers she loved. The taste was one she'd longed for over the past few months. God, had it been that long since they'd shared a bed? Made passionate love? Fucked like there was no tomorrow? Had they ever had sex with total abandon? Was this a side of Dee she'd yet to witness? If so, why had she held back from sharing her desires? If Max had known back then when she'd brought Dee to orgasm it was going to be the last time, Max would have kept her from coming a lot longer than she had. That was on her. Dee seemed most comfortable with efficient sex rather than drawing pleasure from the act. Like everything Dee did, Max sensed she never truly let go so she could really enjoy anything. Dee moaned and she focused her attention on Dee's swollen clit and slick hole.

With each stroke of her tongue, press of her lips, Dee's hips rose to greet Max's hungry mouth. She thought about Dee, the woman she loved, giving herself to a stranger, and what it might mean. Had she already indulged in an offer of detached sex? Then reality set in. Didn't everyone do that at some point in life? Anonymous sex could be cathartic, and she hoped tonight's encounter would be that for Dee. She didn't want to consider Dee was with her because she was trying to purge Max from her memory. For a minute, she couldn't breathe.

"Don't stop." Dee's eyes were hazy slits, just visible in the cut-outs, and filled with the kind of lust Max had often wished she could have seen when they were together. She wanted that kind of total surrender now from Dee, wanted her to fully let go for once.

Max wasn't about to let any opportunity of being with Dee go to waste. Damn her crushed heart. If she had any hope of Dee giving her another chance, she'd better lick her pussy until she couldn't think of anything else. Until she cried out and collapsed in ecstasy. If that's what Dee was looking for, Max wanted to be the one to give it to her. She stared into Dee's blue depths. "I won't," she said. She didn't have to try to disguise her voice. It was choked with emotion.

She focused on the rock-hard clit, alternately sucking and licking. Without even thinking, she slid two fingers into Dee's wet entrance and shuddered when Dee reacted with a long, deep moan. The misunderstanding between the two of them had happened. She could either insist on pleading her case or enjoy where she was in the moment, and give Dee so much pleasure she'd be begging for more. The desire to please her, to show Dee how much she wanted her, was almost as important as showing her how much she loved her. It was what she wanted to do, but more than that, it was what she needed to do. For both their sakes.

❖

Dee's pussy was slick and greedy. Where was this sudden freedom of saying what she was thinking coming from? Had she really just told the woman licking her not to stop? Maybe there was something to be said about sex with strangers. But then, she had gone so long without Max's attention, and it had been so damn hard thinking about someone taking her place, she grasped at any justification for physical pleasure by telling herself it was about time. She couldn't fight the anguish any longer. She needed to sink into oblivion, and she had a feeling Redemption could get her there. This was how she always centered herself, finding steady ground to stand on when Max made her come.

Max's love for her wasn't in question. It never had been. *If Max were here...* That thought flew out of her mind when Redemption slipped her fingers inside. How did she know what Dee craved? Max always knew. Whose body was Max mastering now? Was it that movie star she'd caught Max with, laughing and smiling like they'd known each other for a long time? Maybe they had. Maybe, just maybe, the blonde wasn't the only one.

Redemption picked that exact minute to dance her fingertips against that spot that made her squirm, and she sucked in a quick breath. When she was mentally in that special place she thought of as ecstasy she didn't have to think or worry or pretend. All Dee had to do was be. She'd been in a black hole of regret and longing, but it was time she moved on, like Max had, but the lie pressed against her heart. As much as Max had insistently tried to get in touch with her, it must have meant that she still cared. Didn't it? Could it mean that she missed Dee as much as Dee missed her? But she didn't want her excuses for whatever had happened with the woman she'd seen her with. She couldn't handle that.

Her center grew heavy. Redemption had talent. The only one who'd been able to make her ache to come was… Dee glanced down and met expressive eyes. There was something familiar about them, though the haze of her impending orgasm made thinking difficult. The more she looked, the more guilt overtook her. Her chest tightened. The only woman she wanted to come for was Max. She reached to touch Redemption. To get out of there now because Redemption wasn't who Dee wanted licking her, fucking her. At first glance, from what she could tell about her features that lay under the makeup, Dee had thought she looked a little like Max. She wasn't Max, though. Max wasn't with her in the cabana. She didn't have the chance to tell her to stop. Redemption pressed another a finger to her ass and easily slipped in. Her orgasm closed on her like a runaway locomotive. Redemption kept slowly fucking her holes and using her talented mouth while wave after wave coursed through her, leaving her powerless to do anything but sink into the sensation. The screams she spewed were deep, sorrow-drenched sounds, coming from the part of her brain that was barely functioning. Who was this dark phantom taking her as though she knew Dee's soul? She had to end the encounter she was already regretting and gently pushed her head away. "No more." The ensuing empty feeling when Redemption slowly withdrew matched that of her soul, her heart.

"Are you sure?"

Dee wasn't sure of anything except she missed Max terribly, wishing she could turn back time. How long was she going to lie to herself about what she wanted more than anything in the world? Words like "I'm sure. You aren't Max" sat on her lips. Redemption hadn't done anything wrong. Dee wasn't about to hurt her because she was hurting. All she could do was nod.

"Thank you for letting me please you." Redemption kissed her inner thigh, then rose in a graceful move of pure strength.

Dee got herself together and tried to straighten her clothes. She had to get away from the awkward predicament she was in. Redemption opened the stand next to the chaise and withdrew water, then cracked the seal.

"Please drink some of this."

Grateful for the diversion, she took the offer. "Thanks." Her throat was scratchy from her groans and screams. Dee didn't want to think how many people might have heard her shouts of release. Had anyone cared? Or even noticed? She looked on as Redemption opened a second bottle and emptied half in one swallow. The rise and fall of her throat was erotic to the point that Dee's clit twitched to life, and she did her best to ignore it. She couldn't let anyone take her again. Even if her body begged, she would think otherwise. "You might want to have your paint touched up. There are a few smudges around your mouth." She tipped her head, not knowing why she was staring, except—

"If you're okay, I'll go have it fixed." Redemption took a step back. It appeared as though she couldn't wait to make her escape either.

"I'm okay." She spun her legs around and stood. "Who are you really?" Dee was shorter by a few inches, though she felt like a dwarf in comparison. Tiny and small and inconsequential.

Redemption shook her head. "Just a woman." She pulled the material aside and disappeared.

Dee watched her go and was left behind a curtain of silence

without so much as a good-bye. There wasn't anything else to say anyway. She'd let a stranger touch her and she'd climaxed so hard she'd nearly wept. As much as her guilt wanted to make her feel bad, the whole experience had exceeded anything she could conjure happening if her desires were unleashed. Dee turned away, refusing to feel bad about what they'd both wanted at the time. Redemption hadn't done anything she hadn't consented to. Maybe she'd used her imagination to pretend Redemption was Max, but no one could take her place, no matter how talented they were.

The warm air brushed her skin as she let the curtain fall behind her. Redemption had brought her respite from herself, and she was grateful, though she doubted that was her real name. Just like Redemption wasn't Max, even if there were moments when she'd thought otherwise. No matter how attractive she was. There was only one woman Dee wanted. Redemption didn't come close to her Max. Her eyes burned. *What have I done?*

Dee passed people in small groups as they talked and played with nipples and crotches, avoiding eye contact as much as possible. Who had heard her moans? But no one was paying any attention as she strode by. Why would they? She was one of many who had moaned tonight. Did any of them know Redemption's real name? Why was she so curious about a stranger? Even if Dee knew who she was, it didn't matter. Damn, though, it had felt so good to have an orgasm she hadn't been responsible for.

She needed a drink. The mansion would provide, but she didn't want Tosh's probing gaze, and she definitely couldn't face Elizabeth. She might have already gotten a report from Redemption. Would either of them mention what had happened? Talk about an encounter that took place privately? Dee wanted to believe Elizabeth was a woman of integrity and that she wouldn't tolerate anyone who didn't honor the anonymity rule.

The closest bar was in the pool, and she thought briefly about diving in, clothes and all, but kept going. The laughter that bubbled out of the jellyfish bar to greet her sounded a little maniacal. With emotions running the gamut, Dee put her hand over her mouth to quiet any judgmental remark about the people inside and opted for the main entrance instead. She intended to find another bar where she could get a shot of a libation that would numb her senses. She didn't want to think anymore, like when she'd been immersed in her all-consuming climax. It had wiped out all other thoughts, except one.

The music of a live band drew her to the left, an area she had yet to explore. The wide oak double doors led to a ballroom filled with crystal chandeliers resembling a thousand flickering candles. People danced in a variety of styles, some grinding seductively and smiling; an unspoken promise of more to come was easy to read in their eyes.

To her left was the object of the quest she'd been on. A granite-topped bar with a massive array of liquor bottles filled the tiered shelves. In the background was a lighted mural of a tropical resort where the beach stretched off into infinity, and the palm trees appeared to sway in a silent breeze. Dee breathed out her relief. Tosh wasn't behind this bar, but the muscular butch that was there wore the same vest all the bartenders wore along with the common Zorro mask. She glanced up at the people on the dance floor as she wiped glasses. Their eyes met as she made her way closer and slid onto an open stool. She still felt ill-prepared to order without having her credit card.

"Good evening, I'm Jac. What can I get you?"

She almost blurted out "Amnesia," but thought better of it. "A shot of whiskey."

Jac studied her, put a shot glass on the rail, and poured brown liquid before sliding it in front of her. "I've always found bourbon helps chase away mental ghosts."

Christ. Was she that easy to read? Dee picked the glass up and threw it back, then proceeded to cough as the burn traveled from her tongue to her stomach and exploded in a fireball of heat.

Jac looked as though she were ready to intervene, and she waved her off. She might sound like she was going to die, but she would be fine in a minute. If she was going to die from anything, it would be from her broken heart.

CHAPTER FOUR

Max couldn't move from the shadows as Dee disappeared into the mansion. Two opposite emotions warred inside. Sadness that Dee had let go with a stranger and let her do the things that up until now, only Max had done. What followed was elation that she'd finally gotten to touch her again, feeling her pussy respond by swelling and becoming impossibly wetter. Missing Dee had motivated Max to enlist Elizabeth's help and scheme for Dee to be in the same place as Max, the one thing she hadn't been able to accomplish on her own. Beneath all her internal conflicts, Max sensed a glimmer of hope that resounded in her soul. If the universe was looking at her favorably, there was still a chance for them. Redemption indeed.

A spark flared inside and caught like dry kindling. She wanted Dee in her arms and a thousand other positions that flashed before her. She'd been such a fool. How had she expected Dee to know—really know—how fucking sexy and desirable she was if Max hadn't made sure she experienced that kind of fire each and every day? The realization jolted Max into the present, making each of her steps determined and sure. She would not miss another opportunity. No matter what else happened between them, Max would make sure Dee knew how sexy and desirable she was. The final decision about a reconciliation would be Dee's, of course. Like most decisions had been, like it always would be if she had the chance to be with her again.

As she passed through the jellyfish bar, Tosh frantically gestured her over, and Max made a detour. Guests openly admired her with appreciative comments about the spectacular paint she wore and her physical attributes. She nodded and mumbled thanks as she moved. She had to get to Dee before she left, and she wanted her to know this time, that it was her.

"Hey," Tosh said as she leaned close to keep their conversation private. "Elizabeth wants to meet you at the back staircase."

"I can't. Dee is going—"

Tosh held her forearm to keep her from moving. "Dee's not going anywhere. I've got Jac keeping her busy. Besides, she's shooting whiskey, so I doubt she's in any hurry to go anywhere."

"Whiskey? Dee?"

"Yes, so go see Elizabeth and then you can go do whatever you were going to do." Tosh grabbed a bottle of wine and filled three glasses with the same amount and handed them off. When she saw Max still there, she made a hand motion for her to get moving. She tucked away her shock at Dee drinking anything stronger than a glass of wine. It wasn't something Max had ever witnessed. What else about Dee had she missed? Had she become so secure in their relationship that she hadn't noticed other things? Things that might have contributed to Dee's belief that Max wasn't interested in her sexually or, worse yet, being her partner in life? *Fuck.*

Skirting the mass of people that had grown substantially since she'd gone into the cabana, Max finally made it to the theater. A threesome huddled close, one woman leaning on the wall while a dark-haired woman was on her knees rabidly licking and sucking her center. The fabric of the mask she wore had to be soaked. Another woman's mouth was latched onto one nipple while she tugged at the other. Max squeezed her thighs and moved aside the heavy velvet drapes hanging from the ceiling and cautiously felt her way to the stairwell. Lucky for her, she'd been there enough to have an idea where she was going.

"There you are," Elizabeth said before flicking the switch

that lit the dozen small sconces that showed the way along the staircase. She'd told Max it had originally been used by the house staff of the former owner so they could move from one floor to another without disturbing the guests. Elizabeth had decided to keep it during the renovations and constructed the theater around it.

"Tosh said you wanted to see me." She dispensed with the pleasantries.

"I've found someone to give Dee the winning raffle ticket whenever you make your grand appearance." Elizabeth looked pleased by having solved the issue of how to get a ticket to Dee, knowing she hadn't prepaid the five hundred dollars to purchase one on her own. Elizabeth donated the proceeds to the local LGBTQ youth center.

Max tried not to let her anxiety show. Elizabeth had been generous in providing the invitations, not to mention being instrumental in getting her staff on board. "Thank you." She glanced up the stairs. How long would it take for Dee to grow restless and decide to leave?

"Jac sent me a text two minutes ago that Dee was nursing a shot of bourbon with a seltzer chaser." Elizabeth smiled. "Go ahead. I'll keep an eye on her and make sure she doesn't miss the one person she actually wants to see tonight."

"I don't know how true that is, but I appreciate the vote of confidence." She took the first step before turning to press her lips to her cheek. "Thank you, Elizabeth."

"You've thanked me enough. You're a good friend and I wouldn't have it any other way." Elizabeth drew the curtain back and disappeared.

Max raced up the stairs. Her room was the first one on the right and she gazed into the retinal scanner, ignoring the second of discomfort as the light flashed before the door clicked open. Her tuxedo was perfectly laid out across the bed, her shoes on the thick carpet at the foot. For a moment she forgot she wasn't wearing clothes and began to reach for the clasp of her pants. She laughed out loud as her long strides brought her to the bathroom. A bottle of blue liquid sat on the counter on top of a typed note.

Thoroughly wet skin with warm water. Use a generous amount on a washcloth and work into suds, then apply from the face downward. Repeat as needed.

In the lower right corner was a sentence written in a beautiful script.

Wishing you much success with Dee. We're all rooting for you.

She was warmed by the sentiment. The artists were so professional as they painted her breasts, ass cheeks, and crotch. With three of them working on her, she was done much quicker than she imagined. Then she'd mingled among the guests, some who she knew. No one had approached her with any familiarity, although a few women had lightly touched her.

Max turned on the shower, gathered her supplies, checked for the long-handled brush hanging from a hook, and stepped under the stream. Once she was sufficiently wet, she created a thick lather and began to scrub. Every time she closed her eyes, the months-ago scene at her dealership played. The fateful afternoon when her world went from having it all to having nothing at all, and the look of utter disappointment and devastation on Dee's face was one she would never forget. What made the whole situation worse was Dee's refusal to let her explain. If they did reconcile…

"No," Max exclaimed to the steamy enclosure. "When." She had to believe it wasn't too late for them. She'd always thought they were destined for each other, and she wouldn't abandon that belief no matter how hopeless it might look to others. Giving up wasn't in Max's DNA any more than walking away was. Sure, she'd have to get to the bottom of why Dee had refused to let her explain exactly what she'd seen, but first things first.

Max turned off the water and opened the shower door, gazing at the mirror opposite her. From what she could see, the transformation from stranger to herself was complete. While anonymity had served a purpose, she was ready to move forward with her plans. Once dried, she put on her tuxedo and donned the mask Elizabeth had provided, as promised. It was designed so that the staff knew who she was. Max couldn't begin to show enough gratitude to her. She'd quickly become someone Max could rely on, and she made an oath to herself that she would honor their friendship no matter what happened with Dee. The half-mask was made of soft material and conformed to her face. The outline of red was similar to the shade of Dee's dress, and she couldn't help wondering if it had somehow been on purpose rather than just coincidence.

This time Max headed for the front staircase. She would find Dee, tell her how much she loved her and how she would do anything for a second chance. A chance to not only tell Dee about the commercial rehearsal she'd witnessed, but also how she hoped they could start to build a better, more open and secure relationship. Then, only then, would she be sure Dee knew how devoted Max was to the future and their life together.

As she descended the steps, Max looked at the mingling guests. Some were laughing, talking, or just hanging back to people-watch. Others were engaged in various stages of sexual acts. One couple in particular caught her attention. A woman whose only outfit was her mask and stilettos leaned against a wall, and the other woman wore nothing on top except for the painted illusion of leopard skin, black pants, and bare feet while wielding a black strap-on dildo. The woman in stilettos exchanged places, dropped to her knees, and began to suck the dildo.

Max couldn't help watching as both women appeared to enjoy the attention they were getting, and the gaze of the one leaning against the wall met hers before she shared a slow smile and a nod. She wasn't sure if she was being invited to join them or just acknowledging an unspoken connection. One of her fantasies was being the woman against the wall, with Dee on her knees, sucking the toy she'd bought a few years ago but had never used. Her body was certainly reacting as though she were already taking the leopard woman's place. Max returned the smile and kept going.

From the doorway of the lounge Max admired her beloved. God, how she missed her company, the conversations they shared, and the comfortable life they had. Though, now that she'd taken the time to examine it, maybe shared wasn't an accurate description. They moved in different circles, Max and her associates, Dee and the beauty industry. Like other aspects of their life, each accepted their differences but rarely made an effort to include them in their own. What did that say about their investment in each other or showing appreciation for being individuals first?

Max took a step forward, and her heart sank. A woman dressed in biker clothes with pointed studs on her boots and a lot of leather moved next to Dee and revealed a dazzling smile beneath her half-mask. It was obvious even from where she stood that the woman was muscular. Her height matched Max's and she might even be taller. The air of confidence in the way she moved and how she crossed her ankles as she leaned on the bar told Max the woman was comfortable in who she was and what she wanted. Right now, the biker wanted Dee. Jealousy rose in her like a tsunami heading for the shore, her possessiveness building as she neared her target. Max stood within hearing range, turned away, and stood behind where Dee sat.

"That dress looks really good on you," the biker woman said.

"Thank you." Dee sipped on the liquid in her shot glass.

The woman ordered a martini. "This is quite the party."

"Mmm. Yes, it is." Dee sounded distracted. The biker seemed undeterred by her lack of attention.

"What do you say we wander to the playroom for a bit?"

Finally, Dee perked. "And why would I do that?"

Biker woman leaned closer. "Because I happen to know where all the fun things happen, and I'd like to share them with you."

Dee hesitated so long, Max almost revealed herself.

"Thank you, but I don't think so. I'm not in a very good mood and wouldn't want to spoil your fun."

The woman moved closer and slid her hand into the side slit of Dee's dress. "All the more reason to say yes."

After throwing back the rest of her shot, Dee stopped the woman's hand from moving any further, and Max let out a relieved breath, but her relief didn't last long. Dee smiled as she stood.

"Maybe you're right." She picked up her seltzer. "What's your name?"

"There's no names, remember?" She tapped her mask.

"Right." Dee took a deep breath, then hooked her arm with the woman's. "Show me what your idea of fun is."

Biker woman was practically drooling. Why wouldn't she be? Dee was gorgeous. Even if she couldn't see her face, her body was enough to get any breathing person hot. Max had all she could do to not end the charade and stake her claim on Dee, but the other part of her, the same part that got turned on in the cabana at the thought of Dee having sex with a stranger, now told her to play along as a voyeur. Regardless of her first instinct to step in, another part of her wanted to find out what Dee would be like if she lost her sexual inhibitions, and for that she'd have to rein in her fiercely protective side. She hoped she could, because otherwise she might alienate Dee even further, and that wasn't something she was willing to risk.

CHAPTER FIVE

Dee didn't bother asking again for a name. Everyone was nameless here. The woman beside her looked very different than Max with a solid build, short blond hair, and a playful confidence that she found surprisingly attractive. Tonight was supposed to be about fun. The woman she'd let lick her needy pussy gave her a much-needed physical release, but she'd been lost in lamenting her loneliness. Fun had been the furthest thing from her mind.

They climbed the massive staircase side by side and she paused briefly on the balcony. The front doors had been opened at some point, fully connecting the indoor and outdoor spaces. The sounds of conversation and sultry music, along with moans of pleasure, mixed together to create an unfamiliar language, and she could easily see what the attraction was. People were free to just be. To enjoy pleasures of the flesh and free their mind from the worries of life. If only she could do the same. The woman stopped beside her.

"Should we be up here?" Dee asked.

"It's fine. I've been attending the masquerade from the start. Elizabeth and I are friends." The woman turned and pointed to the hallway to the right. "It's down this way."

Dee didn't give herself time to change her mind. She was determined to enjoy the night and step out of her comfort zone. Maybe if she'd done more of that over the years, Max wouldn't have gone looking. Becca and Jane had vehemently tried to convince her to hear Max out, to give her a chance to explain. But what was there to say?

The woman slid her hand over Dee's ass, bringing her back to the moment as they stepped into a large, dimly lit room. The walls were a dark shade of blue, the lighting muted except for splashes of red. Thick beams crisscrossed overhead in a grid pattern with supporting posts throughout the space. Large eye bolts adorned each one. Another wall was covered in chains and ropes and other contraptions. Dee had no idea what they were used for.

"Have you been to a playroom before?"

Dee hadn't done a lot of the things she wondered about. Of all the books she'd read, she had yet to actually see how other people embraced their sexual fantasies. This didn't look like a place of pleasure, though. It looked like a place of pain. Was this similar to the sex clubs she'd heard about? If she stayed, she was going to find out. "No." Before they went any further, she had to know something. "I can't do this if I don't know your name." Her last encounter had been a gift from the host, but even then, she knew the person's name. "I don't mind if it's made up." What difference would it make? She wouldn't be able to recognize anyone.

The crystal-clear eyes that held hers revealed an undisguised heat. "Harley."

The name tumbled around with her inner voice. It fit. "Hi, Harley." She waited a beat, but all Harley did was keep her attention focused on Dee. "Don't you want to know my name?"

"I already know it," Harley said. "It's Curious." She smiled beneath her mask before giving Dee's hand a little tug to guide her to a massage chair that had been modified with more of the same metal eyes, Velcro straps, and lengths of rope.

What Harley said was true. She *was* curious. The evidence was in the rock-hard, prominent points of her nipples that threatened to poke through the material and the wet heat oozing from between her thighs and soaking what little she wore between them. All she could think about was what Harley planned to do to her. Whatever it was, she was determined to enjoy it. "You're right." She gave a small chuckle. "Charming and clairvoyant. What an interesting combination."

Harley turned as they reached the chair. Her gaze had changed to predatory. "Take off your clothes." The charmer had changed to dictator in a flash.

The time to decide if she was all in had come. She'd promised herself she'd let go, enjoy what was happening. She found the hidden zipper along her left seam, pulled the sleeve off, and dropped the material to puddle around her feet. With her thumbs hooked in the lace, Dee slid her thong off. She was breathing hard, and more moisture leaked from her swollen lips.

"Excellent." Harley's gaze moved down from her eyes to her mouth to her breasts. After hesitating long enough for Dee to know she'd examined each and the tips of her nipples puckered so tightly she moaned, Harley's gaze lowered more as she finished her head-to-foot inspection. Harley took a step closer and crouched onto one bent knee. "Spread your legs."

Dee groaned and hesitated.

"Obey or I end this now." Harley's voice was firm.

Dee widened her stance. She stared straight ahead, shivering. Harley spread her folds before entering her several times, then stood.

"Clean me." She held up two glistening fingers.

Harley's intense gaze held her in place. What was Harley feeling? Was this when her inhibitions and long-suffering actions wrapped around acting with decorum and the kind of social etiquette her mother insisted on ended? Social expectations had followed her into adulthood, and into her and Max's bedroom. Max had tried to encourage her to let go and enjoy their intimacy in whatever form it took, but she hadn't been able to. It was as though the voice of her mother was in her head every time they had sex. No, that wasn't right. She wasn't allowed to "have sex."

She'd been taught that anything other than "normal" sexual activity was deviant and to be ashamed of. Max had been patient with her time and again, but there hadn't been one instance she'd been able to enjoy sex with abandon. Tonight with Redemption had been the first untoward act Dee had gotten lost in, but in the end, that too had been abruptly interrupted by guilt and shame. Dee opened her mouth, stuck out her tongue, and proceeded to lick and suck the shiny liquid from Harley's fingers. She groaned when Harley pulled away. Admitting she wanted more felt like a prison break.

"Chair," Harley said before walking with confidence to the wall of implements.

Dee climbed into the chair. She glanced around the darkened space and gave cursory glances at the few couples who were there using an array of equipment and not paying attention to her at all. Was everyone who came to this party so comfortable with sex that they lacked any degree of modesty? Her current position wasn't something she wanted to dwell on. She turned her head in time to see Harley striding in her direction with a handful of items that included a large black dildo. Anticipation coursed through her. She took a breath and turned away. Was Harley as experienced as she appeared to be? What would happen if she wasn't and Dee ended up being hurt in a way she couldn't recover from? Did she have a good reason to stop or was it simply fear of the unknown that made her question her decision to try something new? Max would have been here to rescue her if something bad happened, if only she hadn't been so hasty in running rather than ask what was going on.

❖

Max followed at a discreet distance. Their destination was going to test her patience to see if she was correct where they were heading. Max's imagination soared as she envisioned all the things Harley was going to do to Dee. If it were not for her growing need to discover what Dee liked outside of the narrow scope of sex they had, she would have whisked Dee away. Admitting Harley might have skills that she knew nothing about was intriguing, but not being the one to discover them also infuriated her.

She hung back in the shadows against an unoccupied wall where she had a clear view of Dee and Harley. They stopped and spoke a few words that Max couldn't hear over the low thrum of music, some primal beat that stirred her blood. Dee dropped her dress, letting it pool at her feet. The thong was next to go. The miniscule fabric she'd slid out of her way earlier had left nothing to the imagination, and a gush of excitement dampened her briefs. Then Dee got on a chair that had been converted for play, and her imagination of what she'd like to use it for went full steam ahead. Harley slowly walked toward Dee, her hands holding an assortment of implements. She inched closer in hopes of being able to hear their conversation better.

"Have you previously engaged in impact play?" Harley smoothed her free hand over the cheeks of Dee's ass.

"No. What does that mean?"

"Before I show you, you'll have to have a safe word. If you say it, I immediately stop whatever I'm doing and the play ends. Understand?"

Dee nodded. "Yes, but what is the safe word, Harley?" She didn't sound nervous at all, which was strange because inside she was a cocktail of nerves and excitement. Harley smiled. Her name fit her, though it was probably not real, just like Redemption's hadn't been real.

"Can you remember 'cupcake' as your safe word?"

"Cupcake. I'll remember. It's one of Ma—my—favorite desserts."

"Good. Impact play can mean a lot of things," Harley said as she set her collection on a small table. "It could mean this." Harley rapidly smacked each cheek, eliciting two gasps.

Max wanted to stop what was happening, but she wouldn't

interfere unless Dee was distressed. The little wiggle that followed the strikes let her know she might have been surprised by the blows, but they weren't unwelcome. Harley picked up a flogger.

"Or it could be this." She swiped the strips across Dee's back before quickly and sharply striking the outside of each cheek. Dee jumped and gripped the edge of the padded armrest, her face a mix of emotions. "Or this." Harley struck the top of each thigh. Max winced.

"Oh." Dee pulled away.

Harley slipped her hand under Dee's crotch. "You act like you don't like the flogger, but your pussy says otherwise." She withdrew her hand, making Dee moan.

The moisture coating Harley's fingers made Max's clit jump, and she wanted to be part of the scene. She slipped her hand inside her pants and barely managed not to moan, or maybe she did, but she was too focused on Dee and Harley to care. Neither seemed to notice.

"I...I don't know." Dee didn't sound upset, just confused.

Harley put the instrument down, picked up a set of padded cuffs, and moved to stand in front of Dee. "I'm going to cuff you. Whatever happens, you need to breathe through it and remember you can stop it at any time by using your safe word. Do you understand?"

Half of Max's brain wanted Dee to stop now, before there was a reason to stop. But the other side, the side that was curious about how far Dee was willing to go with a stranger, affected her in ways that she couldn't deny. At the same time, she couldn't deny how turned on she was. How much she wished she could use a strap-on with her and give Dee whatever she wanted, however she wanted it. Why had they never had that conversation? Where had this lack of inhibition, on both their parts, been hiding?

"Yes," Dee said, her voice strong and sure.

Max was going to get her answer. Whether she liked it or not, only time would tell, and like every important moment of their relationship, the answer lay in Dee's hands. It was the one part of their relationship she hoped wouldn't change. Dee functioned in her controlled, predictable world. What would happen if that was no longer true? She was about to find out.

CHAPTER SIX

The material circling Dee's wrists and ankles was soft, but there wasn't much in the way of movement, which she supposed was the whole point. Cupcake. She could say it at any time. That was something. How had she so easily given in to something she'd only begrudgingly thought about? But she already knew, and it was time to stop kidding herself.

Redemption had been what she needed. Sure, the offer of sex had been exciting, but the other part was the knowledge that she'd said yes because it was an opportunity to escape reality and pretend that Max was kneeling between her thighs. Doing all those wonderous and amazing things she did to her. Through all the times they'd made love, she'd always sensed that Max was holding back. Like there was something just out of reach that Dee was afraid or too ashamed to admit she might also want. It would never do to be "that" kind of girl. She was more than ready to drown out her mother's iron will with moans and screams of pleasure.

"Up." Harley tapped her ass. "Don't get lazy now just when it's starting to get good." Harley put straps around her thighs and another around her waist, forcing her ass out. A smack and a chuckle followed. "For both of us." Smack, smack.

She groaned when Harley's fingers traced her outer lips. Was that her groaning? Harley? Another stranger who was lurking in the dark? Not that it mattered. She said yes this time because she couldn't stop herself from thinking of Max. Maybe what Harley offered was one way she could show Max she didn't need to go outside their relationship to spice things up. The fingers were gone, but Harley's hand was there with sharp, hard spanks to her center. In spite of the internal conversation to embrace these new and different sensations, for a brief moment, she stiffened, then she felt herself gush. She thrashed what little she could, and the spanking continued until she was panting and sending hot breaths into her mask, her inner thighs soaked and her legs shaking.

"Mmm," Harley said. "Your ass is going to be a lovely shade of sexy tomorrow." She smoothed her hands over her cheeks.

Dee waited for the next slap, but it never came, and she let out a breath in relief. She tried to swallow, but her throat was dry. Her mind began to wander. She deserved to suffer. She was naked, tied to a chair she couldn't get out of on her own, and there were people who could see everything she was doing all around her. Maybe some of those people were here for the same thing she was, to push past the emotional barriers and give herself permission to have fun. This was fun. Right? Still, when she gasped in shock and pain at the succession of something firm striking her, she thought maybe she'd simply lost her mind.

Max watched as the paddle made contact with enough force that it sounded like it was coming from some high-tech audio equipment. Dee's gasp was what made it real. Again and again, the strike landed, and all the while Harley spoke about how she could see how much Dee liked it and that she had no plan on stopping until they were both satisfied. After a half dozen blows, Dee's body softened, and the groans of pain became soft moans of pleasure. She knew those sounds intimately, only tonight she wasn't the one causing them.

Max pulled on her large, distended clit, and for a brief time, she too was lost in sensation before realizing Dee wasn't making any sound at all. Something was wrong. She zipped her pants and pushed off the wall. The next time Harley swung, she grabbed her wrist. "Cupcake," she said. Harley's eyes were hazed, confusion at what was happening clearly written on her face. Max didn't care if Dee heard her, though she doubted she had any clue what was going on. Harley looked between her and Dee, then Harley's vision cleared, and she nodded. She undid the thigh restraints and the one around Dee's waist. Max moved to undo her wrists. This time it was Harley stopping her.

"I've got her. She'll be okay." Harley smoothed her hand over Dee's bright red ass cheeks, up her back and down her legs. Dee moaned softly, and Max moved out of the way. Harley picked up a bottle of juice from one of the many buckets in the room before she undid Dee's wrists.

Max didn't want Dee to see her. Didn't want her to see she'd been there the whole time watching. Harley continued to talk to Dee while she helped her out of the massage chair, and Max slipped away, knowing that the next time she saw Dee, she wouldn't hesitate. She would tell her how much she missed her, how much she loved her, and how much she wanted a reconciliation. In the meantime, she was going to find a quiet spot to take care of her throbbing center because the visions of Dee's willing participation had skyrocketed her libido. She knew how to get that under control. Max only hoped her future was as certain.

❖

Dee sat on the leather chair Harley had helped her to. She'd also found a robe to drape over her. Now that the endorphin rush was over and she realized what had happened, her modesty kicked in. She drank the juice Harley pressed into her trembling hands and tried to remember when she'd lost track of what was going on. The bare-handed strikes to her ass had been intoxicating, but the paddle had brought her to another level of pleasurable pain that she didn't think existed, but it did. It was the not remembering part that scared her. "What happened?"

Harley sat on a nearby stool facing her. "Sometimes impact

play is so intense, so freeing, that the world fades away and all that's left is feeling nothing at all but the freedom of not thinking." Harley placed her fingers over the pulse point in Dee's wrist and was silent for a short time before smiling. "No matter what happened to you for those few minutes, you're fine now."

It was hard to remember what she'd been thinking when they'd started. Something had made her retreat into her body rather than her mind, but what had made her go there? Max. She'd been thinking about not wanting to feel anything for a change, the respite she'd been searching for since the breakup seemed within her grasp. The pain of losing Max was what she'd been trying to escape, and she had, at least for a little while.

"You're going to be sore tomorrow. Promise me you'll take an OTC painkiller tonight for the body aches that will show up later, and drink lots of water. Otherwise, you're not going to be able to move in the morning." Harley watched her expectantly, her concern clear.

"I promise." She glanced at the implements on the table. "Am I bleeding?" Did she really want to know?

"No. I wouldn't do that to you. I'm not a sadist. My hand and the paddle inflict blunt force trauma to the tissues, so you're going to bruise." Harley's smile looked wry. "Your ass will be a spectacular kaleidoscope for a few days."

Relief flooded through her. She was lucky she'd picked someone who was considerate, and she didn't want to imagine what might have happened otherwise. Though she admitted she'd been turned on and there was still a lingering thrum throughout her body, nothing had changed. Deep inside, she still ached for Max's touch. "Thank you for giving me a new experience." One she might want to repeat in the future. She shrugged off her robe and put on her clothes, no longer caring who might see her body. "I think it's time for me to go."

Harley stood. It was so hard to tell what she was thinking without being able to see her face. Maybe that was a good thing.

"I hope you found a piece of yourself tonight." Harley touched her cheek. "And that you enjoyed letting go, at least a little."

"I did. Thank you." It was true. She hadn't known how much she needed to let go until Harley had brought her to that point. Harley opened her mouth, as though she was going to speak, but only shook her head.

"Enjoy the rest of your evening."

Dee nodded and turned. She'd only gone a couple steps when Harley called out.

"Don't forget to stay for the drawing."

Dee turned. "It doesn't matter. I don't have a ticket."

"That a shame. It's a great event." Harley winked.

She groaned under her breath, hoping the winking didn't start again.

Chapter Seven

Max went to the closest bar and ordered a shot of whiskey. She'd made a quick detour to the back staircase with the intent of getting off to quiet her throbbing clit, but once she got there all she thought about was Dee and how she'd completely surrendered to Harley. That's what she wanted for Dee to have with her. So, she abandoned her own need.

She had to find Dee, reveal herself, and ask for a chance to right the wrongs between them. The shot sent a line of fire to her gut, waking her from the semi-stupor that followed the scene with Harley. At least Harley seemed to know what she was doing. She was not just some BDSM wannabe, and Max was grateful for that. Max wandered through the bars, theater, game room, and lounges hoping to catch a glimpse of red. The crowd hadn't diminished by much, though the main floor had thinned, likely due to more people being in the pool or catching the entertainment happening in the huge fishbowl outside.

Random trays of partially eaten food were scattered on various tables, but she couldn't think about eating when her heart ached so much at the thought of having somehow missed Dee's departure. If that was true, the whole evening had been a total waste, and all the efforts of Elizabeth and the staff were for nothing. Tosh breezed through the kitchen door while making the last bite of a sandwich disappear.

"Tosh, have you seen Elizabeth?"

Tosh finished chewing and smiled. "Why?"

"I think Dee's left. Last I saw her she was with a woman upstairs, and now I can't find her." Nothing could be worse than not having Dee back in her life. Tosh took her arm and led her to the kitchen door, then cracked it open. Inside, Dee sat on a tall stool next to a stainless steel island. She was talking to one of the staff while she picked at a plate of calamari, one of Dee's favorite dishes after a late night. Her smile lit up the kitchen, and the chef appeared to be just as happy to spend time with her. Who wouldn't? She was gorgeous, and funny, and a delight to be around. Max backed away and Tosh let the door close.

"Aren't you going in?"

Max wasn't about to interrupt Dee, unsure if seeing her would upset Dee. It was best if she let her finish. She'd stand where she'd be sure not to miss her. "She probably hasn't eaten much tonight. I'll wait here."

"You're so in love with her I can't imagine how rough tonight has been." Tosh squeezed her shoulder and strode up the hallway toward the jellyfish bar.

While it had been bittersweet at moments, it was also the first she'd seen Dee in months, and that made it worth the heartache of missing her. Even stopping at the spa unannounced had proven Dee didn't want to see her and had her staff turn Max away. If she could only convince her that she loved her more today than she had yesterday, or last week, or six months ago when her world was still on an even keel. Safe.

Max's head came up. Was that how they'd been living? The comfortable, predictable life of a couple whose everyday activities had become stagnant? No wonder Dee thought she'd gone looking elsewhere. They'd both settled into a routine that served a purpose, but it wasn't how Max wanted to live her life. She wanted to have fun, try new things, meet new people. The life they'd lived was good, but not great. It lacked excitement… spontaneity. Going forward, if given the chance, that was going to change, too. They were young, and it was time they started living the life they were meant to live.

Max waited a little way down the hall, away from the majority of guests. A few very long, very anxious minutes later, Dee appeared. She looked relaxed, though Max could tell she was tired. Dee had experienced quite a night, but she hoped it was long from over. *It's now or never.* "Dee?" she said as she moved closer, her mask still in place.

Dee faced her, her brows knit. "Do I know you?" She stepped closer before she inhaled sharply, her hand at her throat. "Max?" Dee stilled, her chest rising and falling rapidly. "What are you doing here?"

Her eyes filled with unshed tears. Max's heart tore a little more. "I'm here because of you." She stood a few feet away knowing if she went any closer she would have to touch Dee, and she wasn't sure it would be welcome.

"For me?" Dee glanced around as if trying to remember where she was. "I don't know what you want." Her hand fell from her throat as though the weight of it was too much to keep in one place.

She took a step closer. "I want a chance to explain what you think you saw at my showroom." Another step. "I want to have a chance to show you how very much I've missed you." Max stood an arm's length away now. "Most of all, I want to tell you and show you how much I love you."

Slowly, Dee shook her head. "Don't waste your breath, Max." Dee's voice was steady and full of resolve. "Don't you understand? I had to let you go so you could be happy…happier than you were with me."

Another step. "I've been more miserable than I have been at any time of my life." Max touched her face then, sinking into the silky texture beneath the mask. "Please, give me a chance to explain."

The background music paused and a smooth, husky voice called out the number of the winning raffle ticket before announcing their prize could be collected in the theater, and all the other guests could pick up their favors from any of the bars before they left, assuring everyone the party would be in full swing for hours. The music resumed and Dee took her hand, placed a kiss in her palm, then slowly lowered it until they no longer touched.

"I'm not what you need." Dee was about to turn away when a dark-haired woman approached.

"Hi. I have the winning ticket," the woman said as she held it out. "But I have to leave." She shoved the ticket into Dee's hand.

Dee stared at the woman's retreating back, then glanced at Max. "What the hell just happened?"

"You have the winning ticket, but you're not the winner that was announced." Max took her empty hand in her own and gently squeezed. "I'm the winner, and I can show you why if you'll give me a little of your time."

"Now?"

She nodded. "Right now. Please, Dee."

Dee looked at the ticket. "What do I do with this?"

"Bring it with you," Max said as hope coursed through her. At least Dee hadn't walked away like she had that horrible day when her world came crashing down. She'd waited for the hope swelling inside to turn to heartache when Dee seemed on the verge of telling her she didn't want to hear what Max had to tell her. That thought flew from her mind when Dee lifted their joined hands.

"Lead the way."

Max intended to do just that, and she prayed to whoever was listening that Dee would follow.

❖

Seeing Max confirmed Dee wasn't crazy. She *had* caught glimpses of Max throughout the night. Well, maybe she *was* crazy for going with Max, but she wasn't thinking with her head, she was following her heart, and her heart told her that they both deserved to know exactly what had happened between them. Her stubborn streak—the same one that used to get her punished as a child—had kept her from giving Max a chance to explain. It had been a foolish move on her part, but once she'd started justifying her actions, she couldn't stop herself. Couldn't admit she'd gone with a knee-jerk reaction and didn't know how to go back without looking any more ridiculous than she already felt. Once they climbed the staircase located at the back of the house, Max walked beside her.

"You seem quite familiar with this place." The thought that Elizabeth was more than a friend to Max rankled her in a most unpleasant way. Max studied her, her steps slowing until they stopped moving at all.

"If you're asking if I know Elizabeth intimately," Max began before taking a deep breath. "The answer is yes."

Dee felt her heart hammer in her chest and her vision blurred. *So, there's more than one.*

"We have a deep friendship and spend time together at car shows." Max stepped into her personal space. "I've been a confidant and a good listener for Elizabeth. When you're rich, it's hard to tell who's a real friend rather than someone interested in being close to the money." Max's hand found hers. "That's what we have in each other. A love of shared interests, Dee. I'm not sleeping with her." Max lifted her hand toward her mouth and kissed her palm, her tongue drawing a line of fire down the center.

"I'm sorry. I have no right to ask about any—"

Max pressed a finger to her lips. "Dee, I'll tell you everything you want to know. Always." She glanced down the hallway. "Will you please spend the night with me?"

If she thought her pulse was racing before, it was an out-of-control locomotive as she stood glued to the spot in the opulence of Elizabeth's home. She wanted Max's touch, wanted her lips and mouth and fingers playing against her skin and filling her. Then she remembered the painted woman…Redemption…and Harley. She'd gladly given herself over to them, a rare behavior for her, in search of the relief that never came in the darkness of her bedroom. Dee knew the reason she couldn't be at peace was because Max had always been her safety zone. Her port in the many storms that raged in her life.

But Max was so much more than a comfortable place to lay her head. She'd brought joy and happiness at a time when Dee doubted she'd ever find either. What had she given Max in return? Had she been as selfless or as loving as Max? Had she even once reassured her that there wasn't anything they couldn't get through together? Was she so wrapped up in her own self-loathing that she had nothing left to give Max? The one person she should have been devoted to for the pure pleasure of doing so.

"Yes, I'll stay."

"Thank you." Max's forehead crease disappeared, and the sight of her relief nearly broke Dee's heart. Max slowly lowered her hand, and they continued to the last room on the left. Its door was the same as the last half dozen they'd passed. What was surprising was the electronic scanners mounted next to each one. Max pressed her thumb to the pad, and a light flashed before the audible click made her jump. "Elizabeth believes everyone's entitled to their privacy." She pushed the door open and led her inside.

Dee did a slow spin. "Wow." The one word she was able to mutter did nothing to pay homage to the grandeur of the room. A huge four-poster king bed was the centerpiece of the space, though it by no means overpowered the room. A matching wooden armoire stood against one wall, a roll-top desk against another. Double doors led out to what she assumed was a Juliet balcony. Directly across from the bed, mounted up on the wall, was a massive TV where a movie similar to those being shown downstairs silently played. Her gaze was transfixed on the two women on the screen. They were in an inverted sixty-nine position. The one on the bottom wore a strap-on, the other moaning as her partner pumped the dildo into her hungry-looking mouth while her face was buried in the crotch of the woman on top. Dee's center grew heavier and wetter than the very first time she'd seen Max and pictured her strong body over hers in a similar position.

When she could tear her eyes away, Max stood nearby. She wasn't able to interpret the look on her face. It may have been predatory. It could also be a great sorrow that she was battling to hide. Whatever it was, she'd decided during the final steps toward the bedroom that she wasn't going to leave without having answers to all the questions she had been asking herself the last few months.

"Do you stay here often?" The familiarity with which Max moved around the room as she lit candles led her to believe this was far from her first stay.

Max lit the last candle, set down the taper, then slipped out of her jacket. "Elizabeth has been a good friend. Over the last few months, I've made a habit of showing up on her doorstep in need of someone to help me sort out feelings I couldn't define." She stayed a few feet away, her eyes searching…pleading. "If you're wondering if I've been with other women, I haven't, Dee. There's no one I want but you." Max knelt, untied her black wingtip shoes, and slid them off before coming close enough that Dee could smell her cologne and hear her steady breathing. She took off her mask, then reached for Dee's before placing them together on the table. She hadn't forgotten how handsome she was, but seeing her unmasked, the raw animal presence that she was sure Max wasn't aware of grabbed her hard. Her knees threatened to buckle.

"The woman at your dealership. Who was she?"

"Lisa is an actress who was recommended by an associate. We were going to make a commercial for the business." Max took her hand again, as though she couldn't tolerate not having a physical connection. "What you saw was a rehearsal of her buying a car from me."

Dee didn't know where to look. Her gut tightened. Max had never given her a reason to doubt her devotion. The day she'd shown up unexpectedly hoping Max was free to go to lunch, she'd been feeling like she didn't belong anywhere. Seventy-five percent of her clients were young, beautiful, shapely women who made her feel like an ugly duckling, so her mood had been anything but upbeat when she walked into the showroom to find a beautiful blonde—Lisa—in one of the convertibles with Max leaning close and her heart-stopping smile directed at the driver. Now she felt more than a little foolish for having jumped to a conclusion based on her own insecurities. If she were Max, she'd want nothing to do with her, but Max was here, and that had to mean something.

"I'd had a horrible day, but that's no excuse for how I behaved."

Max straightened, pushing her shoulders back, ready for battle. "Did something happen? Did someone hurt you?" Max knew there were a few times when egotistical customers had invaded her space, as though that was going to work. Dee was more than capable of taking care of herself in most situations. Max didn't need to be her knight in shining armor, but she did hope Dee would come to her for support.

"No. Nothing like that." Dee had hired a couple of instructors who ran HIT classes and were experienced at handling uncooperative people. In those instances, she hadn't even bothered to hide her annoyance, especially when someone engaged in body-shaming. That behavior hit too close to home, and she didn't hesitate to call on her staff to escort the offensive customer out. "A few of our newer customers came in that day. They were drop-dead gorgeous and knew it. I didn't handle it well." It was a story she told frequently to everyone but Max, though for some reason that day had been particularly hard for her to believe anyone, including Max, would find her attractive compared to the buxom women who were there for a treatment or a massage. They had the kind of body Dee would never have. She was willowy and slender, with what she considered moderate breasts and a small, shapeless ass.

"Babe, no one has anything on you." Max brushed her hand down her cheek then lightly held her chin, directing her gaze upward. "I don't know what to do to prove it to you except by showing you how desirable you are."

Her lips were soft and firm at the same time. Max always had the kind of confidence Dee lacked. It was one of the first things she'd noticed when they met at a local business networking event. Max's tongue traced her lips before they parted. "I want you. Please let me touch you," she said as she reached for the material that lay on her shoulder.

"Wait." Dee dreaded what she was about to say, but Max needed to know she'd let others touch her, take her, tonight. "I let—"

Max's fingers pressed against her lips, silencing her. "I know."

Dee tipped her head, confused by Max's acknowledgment until she saw a smudge of paint behind her ear. After closing her eyes, she pictured the woman—Redemption—on her knees, between her thighs, licking her swollen lips and throbbing clit until she exploded from all the pent-up emotions she'd been hanging on to like a life raft. But if she slowed her mind and didn't look at the makeup and instead focused on how Redemption felt, her touch, her tongue, her unerring attention to what made Dee melt, she would have known it was Max. The lump in her throat felt more like a boulder.

"You," she said as she moved back, her hand to her throat. "It was you in the cabana." She increased the space between them. "Why? Why would you do that?"

Max reached for Dee's hands and pulled her closer, unable to stand the emotional distance between them that she hoped to close. "Because I needed to touch you, taste you, babe. Like I always have. Like I always will." She pressed her lips to Dee's with the intent to show her what she thought Dee craved. Her lips were exactly as she remembered. Soft and yielding. Full, but not overly plump. Visions of what Dee's mouth could do to her and how she could lose herself in the pleasure of her mouth stole her breath. She didn't want to stop…never had…but she had so much more to tell Dee, and to show her.

"I let a stranger do what you should have been doing." Dee's eyes were watery pools of regret.

"It *was* me."

"But I didn't know that at the time!" Dee tried to pull away. "I…I came in your mouth."

"And you were amazing." Max pulled her into her arms, refusing to let her get away. "You're always amazing, love." There had been days when she'd picked up her phone only to put it down over and over again. Tonight, she didn't have to wonder where Dee was or what she was doing. She was going to show her how much excitement they could have in the bedroom as well as in their lives.

"I've never done anything like that." Dee looked ashamed, but she shouldn't be. It was clearly written on her face that she wasn't in a good place, and sometimes sex with a random stranger provided a needed escape. Max believed that was true for Dee. "I let a stranger touch me."

"There's nothing wrong with seeking release, babe." She held her cheek as she gazed into the depths of her eyes, wanting her to see she meant it. Dee's face flushed.

"I don't know how you can be so calm about it."

"Don't focus on the who. How did it make you feel?" Max asked as she began to slowly slide the zipper down on the side of Dee's dress, her lips pressing along the column of her neck. Dee's hands moved to her shoulders as her head moved to expose her throat and she moaned. "Tell me." She let the gown fall and lifted Dee's breast to her mouth. Her tongue played over the hard nipple the way she directed, then tugged with her teeth, eliciting another moan.

"I...it was exciting. I wasn't thinking, just...God, Max, I can't think when you do that."

"Do you want me to stop?"

"No. Please don't stop," Dee said with a whimper.

Max alternated between Dee's beautifully shaped breasts with dark, prominent nipples that puckered and pebbled when she nipped and tugged. "I love watching you respond." She moved her hand down Dee's center until it covered her mound. Dee moaned as she rotated her hips searching for more. "I want you to trust me to give you what you ask for." She slipped the thong off and drew her fingers downward through the incredible wet heat until she pressed two inside, making Dee rise to meet her in a gasping sob.

"Oh, yes." Dee's hand covered hers.

"Yes, what? Tell me what you want." Max slowly fucked her, filling her over and over, her thumb striking Dee's hard, swollen clit. Dee's silence spurred her to give Dee motivation to be expressive. "Tell me like you told Redemption," Max said, her mouth next to Dee's ear.

Dee opened her eyes wide before smiling. "Harder. Fuck me harder."

Max was happy to oblige, but they were still standing, and at some point, Dee's legs were going to give out. That's what she hoped would happen anyway. With her fingers inside her hot hole, Max backed Dee to the bed, and together they somehow managed to get in without losing contact. She pumped her arm like a piston filling her and asked her, "Like this, baby? Is this how you want me to fuck you?"

Dee clung to her. "Yes, yes." She stilled before crying out. Her body shook with the force of her orgasm, and Max nearly cried along with her from the sheer joy of having Dee in her bed.

She pulled Dee closer and gathered her in the kind of

embrace she hoped conveyed all the words that she wanted to say except for the only ones that mattered. "I love you."

Dee looked up from where she was nestled on Max's shoulder. "I know you do. There have been times when I wondered why."

"You doubted I loved you?"

She struggled to sit up and straddled Max's hips so she could look fully at the most handsome woman she'd ever seen. "No. I doubted how you could love *me*. Why would you pick me out of all the gorgeous women out there?" She waved her hand in the air in a gesture meant to encompass all of them.

Max held her as she rose. "You're a gorgeous woman." She brushed the hair from her face. "I've been trying my best to convince you of that even though you should already know." Max's lips were soft, and the kiss they shared so tender Dee's heart swelled. "I want to show you every day for the rest of my life."

Dee studied Max's face and saw love in her eyes. Like a living, breathing thing that filled all the empty places. Dee had seen that same look hundreds of times, but this time, she truly believed it. "There's only one problem."

Max's forehead creased in worry. "What is it, babe?"

"You're still dressed."

CHAPTER EIGHT

Max didn't waste any time shedding her clothes. Dee had finally not only asked for what she wanted, she'd demanded it. That was new between them, and she was ready to explore what sexual fantasies Dee had kept to herself. She'd always been a responsive partner, but Max wanted to encourage the part of her that craved more, desired more. She took several deep breaths before climbing back into bed.

Lying on her side with her head resting in her palm, Max was fascinated by the lines of Dee's body, as though seeing them for the first time. The soft curve of her chin led to a shapely neck, then to the firm yet supple mounds of her breasts. Her nipples were always erect, but not overly so unless she was sexually excited, like now. At times she was so reserved her level of engagement during their lovemaking was difficult to discern. Max moved her gaze over Dee's sides and stomach. She'd lost weight. The outline of her ribs was more prominent, and her stomach was concave rather than showing a little bulge that Max found so sexy. The realization of how much their split had affected her made her frown. She moved her hand over the places her eyes had been, needing confirmation what she saw wasn't just a trick from the lighting.

"I've missed you, Dee. I've missed your quiet mood and your soft moans." She kissed above each nipple, delighting when they grew. "Tonight, I watched a different side of you emerge."

She pressed her lips to Dee's shoulder while her cheeks turned pink. "I want to bring out that side of you. I want the vixen you let out earlier show herself to me." Max lowered onto Dee, covering her long, slender body.

"Baby," Dee said, breathlessly. "I want that, too." Dee pressed up to meet Max, her fingers digging into her sides.

Max growled low. For all the times she'd made love with Dee, she wanted more from her than passive participation. She covered Dee's mouth with hers and was surprised when her lips readily opened and her tongue thrust inside Max's mouth. The exploration continued until neither could breathe and Dee broke away, gasping.

"God. Where has this side of you been all these years, baby? You've got me so hot." Max slid down Dee's body and greedily feasted on each nipple. Dee bucked beneath her, and she slid lower, allowing her hand to map out the way to Dee's heated center, then slipped her fingertips through the wetness. "I'm glad I'm not the only one turned on."

Dee placed her hands on the sides of Max's face and pulled her up. The gaze she witnessed was so expressive, so loving, Max couldn't speak.

"You've always turned me on, Max Woodbury. From the very first time I saw you." The kiss that followed was slow, passionate, burning like red-hot coals that flared into flames and only came from being stoked for a long time. Dee's gaze bored into her very soul. "I'm sorry I didn't tell you very well how much your attention meant to me."

In that instant, hope for the future rose to the surface like a beacon deployed from a shipwreck. "You can tell me now."

"Do you know what I want?" Dee's thumb grazed her lower lip.

"Tell me," she said as she continued to work her hand between them.

"I want your cock in me, filling me. Please tell me you have one with you."

Max was shocked Dee didn't glance away. A few months ago, she couldn't have imagined her having the courage to say out loud what she wanted, needed. "I can make that happen." She slid her hand away and kissed Dee's mound as she moved off the bed. "One of the perks of Elizabeth hosting is knowing every guest room has an ample supply of toys." Max opened the armoire and glanced back at Dee. "Can I pick?"

Up on her elbows, Dee laughed and nodded. "Why am I not surprised?" She gazed at the array of implements hanging inside. "Yes, you can pick. Don't forget the lube," she said before flopping back, giggling.

This Dee—the liberated and carefree one—made Max's heart beat a little stronger and her libido amp up. She picked out a harness made of soft, supple leather and a dildo that would fill her lover, because that was what she wanted to do more than anything. She wanted Dee to feel so full by being desired, cherished, and loved that she'd never second-guess herself again. Max stepped into the harness, slipped the dildo into the O-ring, and tightened the straps. She gave a few test thrusts into her hand and was satisfied with the result. Then she chose a tube of organic lube and squeezed a little on her finger. While there wasn't a distinctive flavor, it wasn't unpleasant. She could live with that. Max stood next to the bed. "Tell me what you want."

"I want," Dee said as she crawled to the edge, "to lick your cock before you fuck my hole." Her eyes flashed mischievously.

In all her imaginings about what this moment might be like, she'd never once thought about Dee on her knees begging to suck her cock. She moved closer until her thighs rested against the thick, luxurious mattress.

"You're so big, baby." Without using her hands, Dee licked the length. She kissed the tip and something inside Max tightened. Then Dee opened her mouth and closed her lips around the end. If she was taller or shorter, the dildo would not have been in the perfect position, like it was now.

"Fuck." Max's head was going to explode from the view

when she looked down. Watching the dildo disappear into Dee's luscious mouth made her clit pound in response. She couldn't stop herself from thrusting a little. Maybe she was lost in the moment, but she could swear the sensation was as if Dee's lips were wrapped around *her*. So, this was why there was so much hoopla about face fucking. She could definitely see why. She placed her hand on the back of Dee's head. "Babe, you're amazing." Dee moved away and the loss was profound. She'd let her slip away once. Max would not let that happen again. Dee's soulful eyes met hers.

"I'm not sure about that, but I do know one thing." Dee took Max's hand and kissed her knuckles, then pressed her lips to her palm. "You deserve more from life. So do I." She took a shuddery breath. "I didn't want to come tonight. I haven't really been enjoying much in life, and the last thing I wanted to do was go to a party where I didn't know anyone. Then I met people who were strangers to start, but they were kind and helpful. Elizabeth was…insightful, charming." Dee laughed. "I'll never look at a gray-haired woman the same."

Max chuckled. "She definitely has a way of expressing herself." She remembered how Elizabeth had helped her realize how important fulfilling one's desires was in life.

"That she does. I want us to enjoy life, too. In every possible way." Dee took hold of her cock and guided her onto the bed. "And I want to start right here." She yanked a little harder, sending shock waves through her. "Right now." Dee growled and pulled her closer before covering her mouth with a kiss so hot it left them both breathless. "Show me how you want to fuck me." She lay back against the mound of pillows and spread her legs wide.

Max nearly lost it. She snapped open the lube and generously coated the dildo before tucking a thick pillow under Dee. "I want you to feel every thrust and every inch of me." She rubbed her cock between Dee's deeply colored folds, the head nudging her clit each time. When Max pushed her hips forward, slowly filling

Dee, a moan of pleasure coincided with each arch of her back. She was so beautiful, tears stung Max's eyes. She bent lower until their hips met, and she circled her tongue around the stiff peak of Dee's nipple. The surface pebbled. Dee's hand grappled at her head, pulling her down.

"Oh, God. Don't stop, don't stop."

She was more than happy to oblige. They'd made love hundreds of times, but never like this. This time her body's movements weren't carefully calculated. The rhythm of her hips mimicked the motion of her mouth, and Dee began to tremble beneath her. She sat up to watch her cock slowly disappear, then reappear. The shaft glistened in the soft lighting. Dee's eyes were closed, her breathing fast and shallow. "Look at me, babe. I want to see you when you come." Lust-filled eyes met her gaze and Max let instinct take over. She lifted Dee's legs, supporting her, and slowly thrust as deep as she could.

Dee gasped. "Oh yeah. Just like that." Dee's head dropped back, her neck exposed.

Max kissed her throat and ran her teeth along the supple column. When she was done she sat back and withdrew. Dee whimpered. "Eyes open. Look at me." Dee struggled to comply. When she did, Max drove her cock in, eliciting a gasp, and Dee grabbed her wrists. She stopped moving, thinking she'd hurt her.

"Please, please. Don't stop. You're going to make me come." She ground her hips in a circle. "Yes, yes. Harder." Dee had her full attention with her pleas.

She supported her weight on extended arms and pulled back until only the head remained inside. Max's body trembled with the need to fill Dee in so many ways she'd never doubt how much Max wanted to be with her for all time. "Tell me again," Max said as she looked between them, their bodies covered in a fine sheen.

Dee's hands covered her breasts and she squeezed. "Fuck me harder." She moaned, her eyes fluttering. "Please, please. I need to come."

With a deep groan, Max thrust her hips until she couldn't see any space between them, and she rested on her elbows, wishing she could taste her while she fucked her. Dee let out a long, deep sound, the kind that let Max know how close she was to coming. Max's own orgasm edged closer. She wrapped her hands around Dee's shoulders and slammed inside, grunting. Dee wrapped her legs around her back and her cock went deeper still.

"Babe." Dee gasped. "I'm going to come."

Max circled her hips between thrusts. It didn't take long until Dee stilled beneath her, her mouth open in a silent scream. She thrust one more time, and Dee's head fell as her back arched. Her whole body trembled.

"Oh, God." Dee pressed upward until they couldn't be any closer. "So good." Dee grabbed her arms, holding on tight as her body shook with the spasms.

Max held her, wanting to satisfy Dee with every fiber of her being. This was the woman she loved, and the woman she wanted to see expand, grow, and enjoy life to the fullest. She nuzzled her neck, placed kisses on her cheek, and gently covered her mouth. Max wanted to devour her. When Dee stilled, she rolled her hips once more, then slipped out. "You're so beautiful." She moved a curl from her forehead and smiled when Dee opened her eyes.

"What I am is a puddle."

"That might be true, but you're still beautiful." Max hoped they weren't done. She'd been so caught up in Dee's pleas and responses she hadn't come. Her body thrummed with a need that went to her core, she wasn't sure how or what would get her over the edge. She hoped Dee understood she wasn't finished, but for now she was content to hold her close for as long as Dee wanted.

CHAPTER NINE

The last time Dee had experienced this level of safety was an eternity ago. Of course, that was an exaggeration, but it seemed that long. Max had always made her feel that way, even when she'd been full of loathing and self-doubt. She snuggled in tighter to Max's firm, warm body and sighed contentedly.

"Everything okay?" Max protectively pulled her in, her arm wrapped around Dee's middle.

"More than okay." There'd been so many orgasms between them, she'd lost track. The dawn had broken a couple of hours ago, and beams of sunlight fell across their naked bodies. She wanted to taste Max again, feel her tremble and moan in the most erotic way, but her body refused to rouse, and the hour or two of sleep wasn't quite enough motivation. She closed her eyes. Her mind drifted. She was almost asleep when a loud rumble came from her stomach.

Max softly chuckled. "I think your stomach is telling you something different."

Dee tipped her head. "It needs to be quiet. I can't move." She kissed Max's chest and played her fingers over her breasts before continuing on a downward path. Max's hand stopped her progress before she reached the dark triangle of soft hair.

"I appreciate your wanting something else for breakfast, but I think we should shower and join the world for some food." Max pressed her lips to her forehead.

She groaned. "Do we have to?"

"No, but we need to." Max rolled on top of her and gave a couple of slow thrusts between her legs before leaving.

"That's so not fair!"

Max called over her shoulder. "You're the one with the loud and clear breakfast announcement."

Her stomach rumbled again. Dee threw back the covers, resigned that she wouldn't be able to sleep, or do anything else, until she ate. When was her last meal? Lunch yesterday? No, last night. The best calamari she'd ever tasted. But still, no wonder there was a symphony happening in her belly after all the calories she'd burned. She stood in the doorway and marveled again at the size of the bathroom. Whoever decorated it had impeccable taste. The terra-cotta floor tiles had enough texture to keep them from being slippery. The largest wall was covered with a mural of palm trees, blue sky, and sunshine. White subway tiles on the other walls gave a classic, clean look. But the shower was a definite work of art. The half wall of richly marbled tiles matched more of the same along the lower half of a shower large enough for its own party. The upper half was a repeat of the white tiles with gray grout and horizontal lines of the darker tiles halfway to the ceiling.

The most amazing sight of all, though, was Max. She was the real work of art. As she shampooed her hair, muscles rippled along her shoulders. Her arms flexed with bulging biceps. The same ones that had supported Max while she slowly fucked her senseless. Her back tapered down to a moderate waist and her ass cheeks showed no tan lines. Max had been nude sunbathing without her. When she turned to rinse her hair, Max caught sight of her.

"Are you going to join me before the water runs cold?" A knowing grin followed.

She stepped into Max's waiting arms. "I was taking in the view." She pulled Max's earlobe with her teeth before sucking at the water drips, and that simple act was enough to make her wet. Dee guided Max's hand between her legs. "Make me come, baby."

Max backed her against the shower wall and slowly slipped her fingers inside. "Like this?" Max asked. "Or like this?" Max rubbed her clit while her middle fingers continued to stroke her. Claim her. Make her moan.

"Like that." Dee gasped as Max continued at an agonizing pace, but it didn't matter. She was going to come, and she wanted this moment to last a lifetime, just like she wanted Max for a lifetime. She'd been so caught up in her own insecurities she didn't—couldn't—see what was right in front of her. Max loved her and wanted her. Life without Max had been miserable. She'd simply gone through the motions, and not a day had gone by that she didn't think of her. Max slipped out and she opened her eyes to find Max waiting.

"I'm going to make you come, baby, and I want you here, with me, when I do." Max held her breasts, thumbed her swollen nipples. "Tell me what you're thinking."

Tears burned and her breath caught. "I don't ever want what we have to end." The words weren't enough, but that was all she had.

Max's mouth covered hers. Languid. Passionate. "I'm not going anywhere, sweetheart. I've been here the whole time. Waiting. Missing you. Wondering what I could do to show you how much I love you. How much I want you." Max pressed inside with her fingers and stretched her in a magnificent way. "Come for me, baby." Max thrust again, touching her deep, rubbing her fingertips in the place that drove her insane.

Dee clutched at Max's shoulders, holding on as the symphony inside reached a crescendo. Then the dam burst, and she cried out, riding Max's hand and shuddering against her. She was going to fall, and she didn't care. She'd already fallen madly in love with Max. All that mattered was that Max was there to catch her. Max was her safety net, with her now. Forever. She was the one who had needed redemption, and in turn, she would give Max all her love.

❖

Max couldn't have hidden her surprise if she'd wanted to.

"Good"—Elizabeth checked her watch—"morning. It's nice to see you both." She set the newspaper down and picked up a steaming mug, took a sip, then waved at both of them. "Come join me. It's not that often I have an opportunity to share breakfast with my friends." She was dressed in a blue silk robe covered in koi fish and lotus blossoms. The garment was a Japanese kimono and would have been as beautiful hanging on a wall as it was on Elizabeth. Her style was eclectic. Max believed most people thought she was eccentric, and Max saw nothing wrong with that. She was also generous, warm, and open. The world could use more people like Elizabeth.

"You're very kind. Thank you," Dee said before sitting across from her.

Max sat between the two women. "Last night was fun. Thanks again for the invitations." She shook out a linen napkin and draped it over her pants. A waiter appeared at their side with a coffee urn, and she wondered if Elizabeth had somehow summoned him or if he had been standing out of sight.

"May I fill your cup, Ms. Woodbury?"

"It's Max. Yes, please." He poured without spilling a drop, holding a napkin in front of the spout to stop any splashes.

"And for you, miss?"

"Hi, I'm Dee. Coffee would be great." Dee's cheeks were rosy, likely from the royal treatment she was receiving.

"Would either of you like juice? Or something to eat?"

"Glen, why don't you fix a tray so our guests can help themselves." Elizabeth held out her mug and smiled.

"Very good, Elizabeth." Glen topped off her coffee, then disappeared through a door that blended in with the wall covering.

Max couldn't help but laugh. "Do all your staff call you Elizabeth?"

"Of course, dear. That's my name." She turned her gaze to Dee. "If you haven't already guessed, I'm not much on formality. Being respected is enough. I pay my staff well, so there's no reason for them to treat me otherwise."

Dee smiled; her posture relaxed. "I'll have to remember that when it comes to dealing with my staff."

Max placed her hand on Dee's. "More problems at the spa?"

"Not really. Occasionally one or two of the employees forget who the boss is." She looked thoughtful for a minute. "Sometimes I don't play the part either. That needs to change."

"It's important for the people who work for you to be grateful for your leadership." Elizabeth took a blackberry from her plate. "Did you have everything you needed in your room?" The smile they exchanged would have been uncomfortable were it not for the fact Elizabeth was all about comfort *and* pleasure. Another reason why her party invitations were coveted.

"Everything was perfect." Max took Dee's hand and gave a little squeeze, making her blush again.

"Excellent."

Glen pushed a large cart into the room. It had an array of covered dishes, along with a bowl of cut fruit and a plate of pastries. Max's stomach tightened at the aromas filling the space around her. "We have plates of scrambled eggs and sausages, French toast, hash browns, and a delightful bacon and cheese frittata." He smiled before placing two glasses filled with orange juice at their places. "Bon appetit."

Dee lifted a cloche and began scooping. "It smells delicious." She poured warm syrup over her French toast and sausage before closing her lips around a big forkful. "Mmm, so good." She washed it all down with some coffee and was about to repeat the process but stopped before taking her next bite. "What? I'm starving."

"Then I suggest you indulge in some decadence. Life is all about pleasure and enjoying the simple things it offers. Good friends, good food…and lots of sex."

Dee almost dropped her fork. The smile that blossomed was genuine, and Max couldn't agree more with Elizabeth's philosophy.

"Unfortunately, I have a video meeting in ten minutes. Please stay as long as you like." She stood, and so did Max. "You're both welcome here whenever you want. My house is always open. Think of it as a getaway destination when life gets chaotic. Doesn't matter if I'm here or not."

Max hugged her and in a low voice said, "Thank you for all your help, Beth. I couldn't have done it without you." She kissed Elizabeth's cheek.

Elizabeth returned the kiss. "Love can happen many times or once in a lifetime. Either way, I'm happy for you both."

Alone again, Max put some food on her plate. "What do you say we finish eating and head home."

Dee wiped her mouth clean of food remnants. "Your place or mine?"

Max felt her body stir in anticipation. "Doesn't matter as long as we're together and can pick up where we left off this morning."

"I like the way you think, but I want to do something first."

Max tipped her head. "What's that?"

"Go to my apartment and pack a suitcase." Dee moved into Max's arms. "I'd like to move back, if that's okay."

Max pulled her in for a searing kiss until Dee struggled for breath. She chuckled. "Sorry." She thumbed Dee's chin. "Redemption is pure bliss."

EXCLUSIVE CONTENT

Piper Jordan

EXCLUSIVE CONTENT

O kay, so maybe I wasn't spending my time in the most productive way possible as I sat leaning back in my chair, glancing at the ceiling panel over my desk. I was debating whether the latest water stain looked more like a fat cat or two peanut butter cups fused together when my boss, Michelle, interrupted my thoughts.

"This just came for you," she said as she tossed an express envelope on my desk.

I rocked forward in my chair, picked it up, and noticed there was no return address. "What's this?" I glanced at Michelle as though she could provide the answer to my lingering question, but she just shrugged.

"Open it." She motioned with a nod.

What a novel idea, I sarcastically thought as I ripped open the package. A black envelope crafted of thick linen paper the size of a greeting card fell onto my desk. My name was written in a metallic gold script font on the front of the envelope, and the same-colored wax stamped with a "D" sealed the flap. "This can't be." I glanced up at Michelle, whose shocked expression seemed to mirror what I felt.

For the past five years, we had heard rumors about an annual women-only sex party called the Decadence Masquerade Ball. It was held at the private estate of Elizabeth Hathaway, one of Las Vegas's wealthiest and most eccentric locals. According to the grapevine, the party was an invitation-only event, and those lucky enough to be invited were sent a black envelope sealed with a gold wax stamp.

As one of four reporters for *What's Buzzin'*, Las Vegas's only website that highlighted everything and anything that was happening in Sin City, I had spent the past few months trying to figure out a way to get my hands on an invitation to this year's ball. But even my most well-connected contacts didn't have enough pull to score me a ticket, which was weird because they monitored the pulse of this town and collectively knew everyone who's anyone. If ever I needed to get into any event, party, or club, they were my preverbal ace up a sleeve. For a fee or a favor, they always came through for me. This was the first time none of them could deliver on a request.

Because of that, I ended up resorting to something that I've never done before...I began begging. A simple online search netted two local for-profit corporations where Elizabeth Hathaway held positions on their board of directors. I left several pleading messages letting her know, in so many words, I was seeking an exclusive invitation to interview her at her upcoming event, hoping she would understand the meaning within the message. But four unanswered weeks had gone by, and my hopes for attending this year's ball had all but faded.

I broke the wax seal and pulled out the card within. On the same style of black linen paper, written in the same metallic gold script, was a simple message.

You are cordially invited to attend the sixth annual Decadence Masquerade Ball. Clothing style and choice is up to your discretion, but in true masquerade fashion, masks must be worn the entire time you are in attendance.

Below that was an address, a QR code, a date and time, and a final notation in small print that stated for the privacy of the guests, phones and cameras were strictly forbidden inside the event.

Wait...back up.

I glanced at Michelle and handed her the card. "This is for tonight." I activated my phone. "In two hours."

"Two hours? Have you finished your article?"

"I was just wrapping it up when you interrupted my creative flow." Which obviously wasn't true. I was still about five hundred words shy of finishing a thousand-word story on the opening night party at the newest members-only club, nestled on the top floor of one of the Strip casinos. I was there until three this morning, and because of that, an article that I could normally crank out in about two hours was taking all day to write. Falling asleep, drooling on my keyboard, and staring at a water stain pretty much rounded out the list of things I'd accomplished in the past eight hours. I sighed. Guess the times when I could pull an all-nighter and still work a fully productive day were gone. At thirty-eight, I feared I was becoming a washed-up partygoer, which if true, would definitely put a damper on a job that required covering events at venues known for catering to the *party till you drop* kind of crowds.

I should have called in sick and slept the day away, but Michelle insisted we turn in a story the day after the event so we could ride on the coattails of the buzz, hence the name of the website. She always said *What's Buzzin'* was the reader's ticket into an opening night or exclusive event that they would otherwise never have access to. And because we gave the reader the good, the bad, and the bizarre of everything we covered, within twenty-four hours of the event, our fan base was over a million followers strong and growing.

"Oh, is that what you were doing?" Michelle snorted.

"Yes, that's what I was doing, and don't be judgy," I shot back, feeling defensive at her tone. "It just so happens I was looking for inspiration for the closing paragraph when you waltzed in here." When cornered with the truth of my incompetence, I will admit there are a few times when I default to lying. Not wanting a work-related lecture from my boss was at the top of that list.

"Okay, send what you have over to Todd, and I'll have him

finish it up for you." She stabbed a finger at me. "You need to get to that ball."

"Todd?" I choked on the name of my nemesis. The just-out-of-college kid who recently wooed one of my contacts into putting *his* name on the opening night list for the latest Cirque Du Soleil show instead of mine. Then he had the audacity to write an article that was viewed and shared over a thousand times more than any piece I've ever written. "Todd," I repeated with maximum disgust as though his name was laced with poison.

"Yes, Todd. He's a fast writer and he can crank it out. I need that article posted by end of day."

"But this is *my* story. I had to pull several strings and promise to take someone who I'm not particularly fond of out to dinner for payback, just to get my name on the opening night guest list."

"Well then, I'll make sure your name's first in the byline."

"You do realize you're killing me with those words." I cupped my hands over my heart and bent forward in mock agony.

Michelle chuckled. "Okay, okay. Let me talk to Todd and I'll let him know that he won't be sharing the byline on this one. This'll come in as a favor."

"I refuse to be beholden to that creature," I scoffed.

"That *creature* is what's going to get you off the hook and out of here so you can attend one of Vegas's most talked about and secretive parties. You do realize there's never been an article written or picture posted of that event. Your story alone will put you and this website on the map, and if you can score an exclusive interview with Elizabeth Hathaway tonight, you will probably be invited to every event in this town from here on out. Without ever having to call in another favor."

Okay, of all the foreplay words Michelle could have used to get me off, those were the ones. I thought of myself as a damn good reporter and had high hopes of one day graduating from *What's Buzzin'* and writing for a major entertainment conglomerate in Hollywood. "Hmm, since you put it like that, I must say that I am suddenly feeling a fondness toward Todd," I said and paused for effect. "Okay, deal, I'll send him over what I have so far, with notes, and he can finish it off."

"Good, now get out of here. I want your story on this ball turned in by end of day tomorrow. In fact, sooner than that, if possible. We could increase our readership by twenty percent with a featured article about what goes on at that party. Now go, get outta here while I fill Todd in." Michelle turned to leave. "And get me that exclusive," she called over her shoulder as she left.

I sent Todd my file, and it pained me to type the words *Thank you, I owe you one* in the email. As soon as I hit send, I picked up the invitation and wondered again who sent it. Whoever it was, I owed them big time. I tossed the card and my laptop in my backpack, shrugged it on my shoulder, and jogged for the elevator. An intern whose name I couldn't remember called out and wished me a nice evening. And as I returned his sentiment, I inwardly smiled and thought, if you only knew.

I hit the well-worn button to summon the elevator, and seconds later, I pushed my body into the packed container of people who grumbled a bit as they made their coveted personal space a little smaller to accommodate me and my bulging backpack. I settled into a designated spot, whipped out the phone from my back pocket, and became one of the silent herd as I stared at the device. Three floors later, I had my key fob in hand as I sprinted across the lobby to the parking lot.

I incessantly pressed the device until the orange lights on my black Jeep blinked twice to let me know it had unlocked the doors and was awaiting my next command. I tossed my backpack on the passenger seat and hit the ignition button. Within minutes, I merged with the rush-hour traffic and headed south on the freeway.

"Siri, call Severely Sexy Sandy." I announced the name my best friend had changed in my contacts list one drunken night. "It suits me better, don't you think?" She had giggled as she handed the phone back to me. "Actually," I'd told her, "it does."

"Hey, girl," Sandy chirped on the second ring.

"Hey, Sandy, I have a huge favor to ask," I said as I slowed to half the maximum allowed speed because rush hour was definitely not rushing.

"Sure, what's up?"

"You'll never guess what I got today," I said in a singsong way.

"A puppy!" I could hear the hopeful happiness oozing from her voice.

I chuckled. It's true, I had been doing a lot of whining lately about wanting another dog. It had been almost a year since Henry, my terrier mutt companion of sixteen years, passed away, and Sandy was by my side as I said my final good-bye through buckets of tears. "I wish, but nope. I scored an invitation to the Decadence Masquerade Ball."

"Shut. The. Fuck. Up. You did not."

"Oh, yeah I did." I smirked as a car darted into the small void in front of me, cutting me off. I hit my brakes, honked, and in return got flipped off.

"How'd you pull that one off?" Sandy's voice softened my momentary irritation and brought my mind back to more pleasant thoughts.

"Some anonymous kindhearted soul sent me an invitation."

"That's mysteriously exciting."

"I know, right? But the deal is…the ball's tonight." I glanced at the digital clock on my dash. "In an hour and twenty-three minutes, to be precise, and I'd like to have my ass there when it starts. So, I was wondering if I could swing by and borrow one of your fabulous masks?" Sandy had once worked in the costume department for both *Mystere* and *Jubilee*, and she had several outfits from the shows tucked away in her closet. Every year for Halloween we dusted a couple off and hit some of the popular parties on the Strip, looking sexy and fabulous if I do say so myself.

"Oh, my God, I have the perfect one for you," she squealed.

"Great, I'll be there in about twenty minutes. And thanks, Sandy, I owe you one."

"I want lunch at Bernie's and a full description of everything you see and do tonight. And I mean complete and detailed. No dancing around the juicy stuff."

I chuckled. "Well, don't you have a kinky little voyeur side that I never knew about...and deal." I had no intention of participating in the sexual side of tonight's party. I was going as a reporter, on official business, with one goal in mind. Which meant the only way I wanted to score tonight was with an exclusive interview with Elizabeth Hathaway. Without it, the article wouldn't get the attention I needed to hopefully elevate me to the next level of my career.

"Okay, see you in twenty," Sandy said as we signed off.

I let out a long breath and tilted my head from side to side to release the anxiety. If the traffic continued moving at the current pace, it would make getting to the ball on time a bit tight. After Sandy's, I still needed to head home, shower, and change. I loosened my grip on the steering wheel, told Siri what music to play, settled deeper into my seat, and hoped the traffic gods would work some of their magic and ease the swelling sea of cars.

By the time I made it across town to Sandy's house, my twenty-minute guesstimate had taken closer to forty-five. A few big-ticket events that were slated for this weekend meant the city was busier than usual, so the ebb and flow of traffic was more like a continuous ebb.

I screeched into Sandy's driveway, threw the Jeep in park, and bolted out of the vehicle. Her door was unlocked, and she was standing in the middle of her living room, waiting for me with the most spectacular peacock feathered mask I had ever seen dangling from her fingers.

"Holy shit, Sandy, it's beautiful," I said as I shuffled over to her. The iridescent blue and green plumage glistened as she displayed the mask in all its glory.

"I know. You are totally getting laid with this on tonight." She handed me the mask. "Try it on. I have another that's a bit smaller if this one doesn't fit."

I pressed the soft fabric against my face as I pulled the strap over my head. After a slight adjustment, we both concluded the fit was perfect. "Do I look like a Vegas showgirl?"

"To repeat…you are totally going to get laid tonight."

"Well, Michelle wants an article written by tomorrow, so it'll be all business while I'm there."

"Oh, please. You're not just going to a sex party, you're going to *the* Decadence sex party. You and I both know the rumors around that ball. The only business that's going to happen tonight is the business of pleasure."

I smiled. Sandy always did have a way with words, and truthfully, I had to admit that the thought did cross my mind a time or two. But A: I had never been to a sex party, so I had no clue what to expect, although it didn't take a rocket scientist to fill in the blanks. And B: I had never had anonymous sex with anyone before, so the thought of participating in anything tonight terrified as much as excited me.

"What are you wearing?" Sandy's question snapped me back to reality.

"I thought I'd wear black jeans and a black button-up collared shirt," I said as I pushed the mask onto my forehead. "Why, what do you think I should wear?"

Sandy paused in thought as she looked me over like a tailor sizing up a client. "Yeah, black on black is always classy. Plus, it won't distract from the colors in the mask."

"That's what I thought, too." It wasn't at all what I had been thinking, but black has always been my default color, since it had been pointed out to me by more than one lover that I seemed to lack the fashion and color pairing gene.

"Okay, take lots of pics and send them to me."

"Can't. The invitation said that for the privacy of the guests, no cameras or phones are allowed into the ball."

"Damn, sounds like there's going to be some kinky-ass shit going down tonight. You are so lucky."

I knew Sandy meant that comment in a sexual way, but I couldn't stop obsessing over the fact that tonight could really help turn my career around. Not that I didn't like working at *What's Buzzin'*, the job definitely came with its perks, but my dream had always been to write about red-carpet-worthy events, instead of the opening of Vegas's latest bar, club, or show.

"Yeah," I replied as I shed the mask and smiled. "I'm sure it'll definitely be a night to remember."

As I showered and shaved the three-day stubble off my legs, Sandy's words about getting laid echoed in my head and sent goose bumps and a shiver up my body. How long had it been since Monica? I began doing the math in my head and stopped when I realized it had been over two years since the breakup, and somehow that just seemed sad and pathetic.

"Wow, two years," I said as the reality sank in that the only one who had been stimulating my body since then was me. Well...and a device or two, but still, how depressing was that? Maybe it *was* time to get laid, and *maybe* tonight would offer more opportunity than just a career move.

I was out of the shower in record time, because yes, I'm one of those who can stay in there singing showtunes until the hot water runs out and my nipples lock in perky status. I peeled back the curtain, and a layer of steam followed me over to the mirror. With one swipe of my hand, I cleared the reflective glass enough to successfully navigate scrunching a palmful of mousse through my short black hair. I pinched at the uneven strands and was reminded how pleased I was with my recent decision to have my long hair cut into a super short and messy style. I loved the new me,. and Sandy said it brought out my inner butch side. My family, on the other hand, hated my new look and constantly reminded me how much they missed my long traditional Hawaiian hair. I smiled as I shuffled toward the closet. "It's called the real me finally looking as butch on the outside as I feel on the inside."

In the next five minutes, I tried on four pair of black jeans, two different styles of black boots, and three black shirts that truthfully, I couldn't tell apart and wondered why I owned so many duplicates. I finally nodded my approval to the bedroom's full-length mirror, grabbed my phone, and checked the time. Shit, the party started thirty minutes ago. So much for wanting to be there on time.

I locked up my apartment, hustled back to my Jeep, and entered the address on the invitation into my map's app. The bubbly female voice skillfully guided me across town and into an exclusive development speckled with mini mansions and impeccably manicured lawns. Sandy called these types of areas the Better Homes and Gardens than you'll ever have neighborhoods, and I let out an envious sigh as I drove past each house, because her little saying was right. No matter how hard I worked at *What's Buzzin'*, I would never be able to afford a place like these.

"In one hundred feet, turn right." The woman's voice reminded me to pay attention and stop gawking at the homes as though they were a set of shiny keys being dangled in front of a toddler...but I couldn't help it. A girl could dream, right? After all, wasn't that what Vegas was all about? And like everyone else in this town, I had my share of striking-it-rich fantasies every time I placed bills in a machine or flopped them down on a table. But unfortunately, my relationship with Lady Luck had always been a bit tenuous, at best.

"Turn right."

I did as I was told and pulled onto a road laced with not-so-subtle signs designating the street as private and that all trespassers would be prosecuted. "This must be the place," I said as I hit my high beams and slowly followed the pavement as it wove up a steep hill. A half mile later, I slowly glided up to a call box in front of a huge wrought iron gate and powered down my window. A sign attached to the box instructed me to hold the QR code on the invitation up to the scanner. I did as I was instructed, and a moment later, I heard a loud click. As the gates slowly swung their arms open to welcome me, I took advantage of the moment, put my mask on, and checked myself in the visor mirror. "Okay, Elizabeth Hathaway, time for your exclusive," I said as I drove into the unknown.

Small white lights recessed into the road turned on as my tires drove over pavement sensors. I had to admit, as I headed toward the house, that the effect was pretty damn cool. Moments later, I was rounding a well-lit stone fountain of four rearing horses that could rival any statue I've seen at Caesars Palace. Colorful flowers arranged in the shape of two overlapping masquerade masks were planted at the base of the fountain. "Nice touch," I said as I slowed in front of the estate.

The mansion was a two-story stucco and stone masterpiece that looked like something out of *Architectural Digest*. Designer accent lights were tastefully interwoven around the grounds to give the landscaping an elegant effect, and a black mask was projected on the one wall with *Decadence* written in gold script underneath.

"Please pull forward." A woman in a tux with a Zorro mask wrapped around her head waved me over. I did as she instructed until her beckoning hand signaled me to stop. I threw the Jeep in park and opened my door as she approached.

"Welcome to the Decadence Masquerade Ball. Please leave your keys in the car so that I may valet your vehicle."

The instructions of the soft voice sounded like a faraway serenade, as my full attention was focused on the double D–sized breasts that were inches from my face. Her shirt was open and barely, and I mean barely was a generous word, covered her breasts. The shirt lacked buttons and instead had two slits on either edge of the fabric where her erect nipples were poking through. Silver nipple piercing rods were used to lock them, and the shirt, in place. Even I had to admit, that was a genius if not a notably painful way to keep from having a wardrobe malfunction.

The clearing of her throat made me glance over her breasts and up to her smiling face. "Here's your ticket," she said as she extended her hand. "If you lose it, no worries. Just describe your car upon leaving and I'll retrieve it for you."

A bit embarrassed at my breast gawking, but not really, I nodded as I pinched the ticket from her hand. She backed away and held the door, allowing me to stand and exit my car. I slipped the ticket in my front pocket.

"My name's Ruby. If you need anything at all, or have any further questions, just let me know," she said.

"The perfect name," I said under my breath as I returned my gaze from her face to her ruby red nipples and lingered a few more moments as I admired the view. After all, first impressions were everything, and so far, this party was definitely making an impression.

"Please take your invitation with you and proceed to the kiosk..." She pointed to a tent that sat to the left of the entrance. "Lisa will instruct you from there. Again, welcome to the Decadence Masquerade Ball."

"Thank you," I repeated, because what else could I say to the Double-D Diva with the ruby-colored nipples that were begging to be noticed?

I strolled over to Lisa, who wore the same tux and style Zorro mask as Ruby, but to my disappointment, her shirt was properly buttoned.

"Good evening and welcome to the Decadence Masquerade Ball. My name is Lisa. For the privacy of those participating in tonight's event, we request no photos be taken, so I need you to place your phone and any other belongings you don't want to keep track of in one of our lockers."

I glanced at the block of colorful small keyless square lockers that reminded me of my high school gym days.

"Your possessions will be safe, and if at any time you need to make a call, your belongings will be at your disposal. But while in use, we request you stay out here and away from the guests." Lisa waved her hand toward the driveway.

I nodded, picked locker number twenty-three because that was my birth date, and hesitated a moment after I grabbed my phone. That little device was like an appendage, and a bit of anxiety swept through me knowing that for the next several hours, I would be without it.

"Once you have secured your items in the locker, please proceed to the entrance, where Shelly will take your invitation and escort you in."

I gently placed my phone on the metal shelf, tapped it twice as if reassuring it that I'd be returning soon, and said a mental good-bye to my adult binky as I closed the locker.

"Right this way." Another tuxedoed female Zorro piped up.

I followed the gentle serenading voice up the two marble stairs and between massive stone statues of lions that sat flanking the front door.

"Good evening, my name is Shelly. May I see your invitation please?" She extended her white-gloved hand, and I graced its palm with the black invitation card. She whipped out a scanner, zapped the QR code, and nodded her approval.

"Please follow me," she said as she ushered me into the estate.

At first glance, it felt like I was entering a high-end nightclub. The lighting was dim and there was a pulsating, but not overbearing, dance music playing in surround sound that set the vibe. I automatically bobbed my head to the beat of an unknown song as I followed behind Shelly. The entryway flowed into a ginormous great room that was two stories high, with polished marble floors and a staircase on either side that formed an elegant balcony that split the space.

"Guests are welcome in all rooms except the master suite upstairs." My escort pointed up as we walked under the balcony. "The pool and Jacuzzi are out those doors." She waved to the right as we entered the great room. The floor-to-ceiling glass doors were slid into the walls, allowing the outside and inside to become one. "There are five bars inside and a total of three outside. Several mobile carts will be staffed by crew members and in rotation throughout the night, but the drink selection on those will be limited. The kitchen is to your left. Please let them know if you have a certain dietary request or wish the chef to make you anything other than what's on the trays of food scattered throughout the estate. The game room, theater, gym, bowling alley, and other various," Shelly cleared her throat for emphasis, "rooms are to the left and right respectively, with signs on the doors that designate which room is which. There's a body painting tent set up on the lawn, and a couple of local performers are about to begin their show just to the right of the pool. Oh, and a raffle will take place in…" She turned her wrist and tapped her watch. "Approximately two hours."

"Oh, yeah? What's being raffled off?"

My Zorro goddess smiled her pearly whites. "The promise of romantic allure and forbidden fruit."

"Wow, what a thing to raffle off."

"Not a thing…a who, and from what I've been told, an evening with her will be most memorable."

I swallowed loudly as my brows shot up.

Shelly chuckled. "Anyway," she continued, "my suggestion to you is to start over there"—she pointed to the left—"at the jellyfish bar. Grab a drink, lose any inhibitions, then go explore. If you need anything, just ask anyone dressed in a tux, wearing a Zorro mask and a gold D pinned on their jacket," she said as she tapped her lapel. "Do you have any questions?"

"Yeah, where can I find Elizabeth Hathaway?"

Shelly paused before answering. "Elizabeth's around."

Okay, wow, could that answer be any more vague? "Well, would you mind pointing her out to me?" I had seen pictures of Elizabeth online, but none that had been taken recently. The last photo was over ten years old, when Elizabeth attended a fundraiser. Her hair was black and shoulder length, her figure thin, and her clothing style colorfully eccentric. But, in ten years' time, as my mirror so rudely reminded me, so many physical characteristics change.

I exhaled a frustrated breath as I glanced around a room of hidden faces. Unless someone helped me out, tracking down Elizabeth at a party that was all about secrecy and anonymity was going to be equivalent to finding a needle in a haystack.

"She's wearing a black mask. I'm sure you'll find her. Again, welcome to Decadence, please enjoy your evening." Shelly turned before I could pepper her with further questions as she retreated to the entrance, where she greeted the newest arrival.

"A black mask," I said as I looked around the room and noticed practically every guest in attendance was wearing some form of a black mask.

So much for a first attempt at tracking down the mysterious Elizabeth Hathaway.

Suddenly feeling a little self-conscious standing in the middle of the room by myself, and not quite ready to begin a full-on stalking of Elizabeth, I decided I could use a drink. Maybe three. After all, didn't Shelly say something about losing my inhibitions?

The jellyfish bar was aptly named. An aquarium was built into the wall the height of the room and length of the bar. At least two dozen large jellyfish methodically swam in the tank lit with a variety of multicolored neon lights that illuminated their bodies. Their slow up-and-down motion was peaceful and mesmerizing to watch. I snagged one of the dozen bar chairs and bellied up to the marble counter.

"What can I get you?" the Zorro-masked bartender said as she placed a black cocktail napkin in front of me.

"Glass of red wine, please."

"Merlot, Pinot, Malbec, Cabernet, or Syrah?"

"Pinot." I smiled, and in seconds she had bottle in hand and was pouring. "Thank you." I took a sip, nodded my approval, then followed with an open-throated gulp that consumed half the glass. She had it refilled the moment I placed it back on the bar. "Thanks."

"You're welcome. Anything else I can get you?" she asked as she corked and returned the bottle to its rightful place.

"Well, actually, I was wondering if by chance you know Elizabeth Hathaway?"

"I might," the not-so-talkative bartender said ambivalently.

"Could you point her out to me, or at least tell me what she's wearing?"

"Sure. She's wearing a black mask."

"So I've heard." I frowned. "Another hint would be appreciated."

She shrugged.

"Yeah, okay…got it." It was obvious she wasn't going to give me what I wanted. "Thanks anyway," I said as I grabbed my glass, launched myself off the barstool and wandered back to the middle of the massive room. I spun in a circle taking in the overstuffed furniture and art décor. I had never fancied myself as an admirer or connoisseur of art, but there were two things that stuck out about the dozen or so paintings that graced the room. First, they were all framed in rather gaudy and oversized antique gold wood frames that dwarfed the canvasses they were meant to highlight. As though the frames themselves were the masterpieces. Second, some of the ones with women as the focal point were stunningly beautiful. I wondered if any of the artists had poster-sized prints that were available for the budget-conscious consumer. I habitually reached for my phone to capture the one that caught my attention the most and was instantly reminded by the lack of bulge in my back pocket that it was no longer in my possession.

"Mmm…" Someone moaned as she placed her hand over mine and squeezed. "Need help with that?"

I startled and spilled some wine. "No. I mean, thanks, but not right now." I smiled at the woman in a red-with-white sequined mask as a feeling of bashful heat flushed my cheeks.

"Well, that's too bad." She leaned in and whispered the words up my neck as she continued a firm grip of my ass. "Because I'm really good at giving exactly what you ask for."

Goose bumps tickled their way up my skin. If there was one thing I enjoyed while making love, it was my lover grabbing my ass while I was on top of her. "Maybe later," I squeaked out through a crackle in my throat because I was still a bit uneasy with the whole anonymous sex thing.

The woman made a tsk-tsk sound as I felt her grip release. My eyes caught hers as she sauntered away, then threw her head back in animated laughter.

A staff member approached, wiped up my spill, and handed me a replacement glass. "Thank you," I said in appreciation of the attentiveness as I transferred my attention to her. One thing was for sure, the crew that was hired for this event was top notch. I made a mental note to give them a nice plug in my article. I thanked her again, and with refreshed wine in hand, I scooted my back against a wall, exhaled a long breath, and tried to be as inconspicuous as possible as I switched to a reconnaissance mission. If I stayed in the shadows, watched, and observed, the elusive host would surely make her presence known.

"Good plan," I said to myself, and as I raised my glass to take a drink, an aggressive bump sent half the wine spilling down my fingers.

"Are you shitting me?" I grumbled in a flash of irritation as I wiped the dripping red liquid off my hand and onto my jeans. I turned to confront the person responsible but froze when I realized not one but two women were the culprits. The one in a blue mask had pressed another, who was wearing a gothic-styled skirt, lacy black mask, and black biker boots, against the wall and was desperately trying to hook the woman's one leg around her waist, hence what knocked my arm, and was still bumping up against me. My sudden annoyance was replaced with a healthy dose of voyeurism as I stood in stunned silence as the black-masked woman tilted her head back against the wall and began moaning, "yeah baby, harder…faster." I glanced down at the pumping motion of the blue-masked woman's hand that was now draped under the other's skirt, and wondered just how much *faster* she could go. I mean, holy fuck, the woman's hand was moving at such a frenetic pace that I expected smoke to start emitting from under the one woman's skirt. And just as my mind began wandering down some pretty twisted roads, the black-masked woman squealed in obvious delight, and I smiled because her orgasmic release reminded me of the sound Sandy's cat makes when she's hungry.

"I, uh…" I stumbled with words because at this point, I was so turned on that the blood flow had left my brain and drained to another part of my body. "I think," I said as I tried to form a complete sentence, "I'll just leave you two to, um, enjoy the rest of your evening on the wall, while I go…" I briefly closed my eyes and tried to put aside thoughts of what it would feel like to be fucked like that. "Um…outside over there and…yeah." I pushed off the wall and began shuffling away as the women came together in what looked like a deep and passionate tongue-locking kiss. "This is me heading outside," I announced to no one as I downed what was left of my wine and placed it on a mobile minibar cart a staff member was pushing past.

I shook out my legs as I acknowledged the wetness that was seeping into my underwear. Now that I was completely aroused, it was time to find Elizabeth, get the interview over with, then start enjoying what this party really had to offer.

I adjusted my mask, for no other reason than to distract myself from a sudden ache that was demanding my attention, and headed outside. The pool was, of course, just as grandiose and spectacular as the rest of the house. It was obvious that Elizabeth Hathaway not only had wealth but loved to display it in all its grandeur. Huge, well-placed, and beautifully lit boulders created the perfect backdrop for a cascading waterfall, which filled a pool that was as large as any I'd seen at the local resorts. Several guests, wearing only their masks, were sitting in the shallow section bellied up in waist-deep water to a built-in bar that could easily accommodate a dozen people.

"If you'd like to go in…" A soft voice made me turn. "You can put your clothes in these lockers. We also provide beach towels." I glanced at a tall Zorro woman with sparkling light brown eyes as she gestured toward a row of lockers and stacks of folded colorful towels.

"Uh, no, not now, but thank you. Maybe later."

A nod signaled she understood. "Well, I'm here if you need…anything." She licked her lips and winked.

"Actually, there is…" I was about to ask her if she could point out our illustrious host when something caught my eye. A huge glass bowl filled with water sat on the lawn just to the right of the pool, and two women who had obviously already checked their clothes into a locker were performing an act that was right out of a Cirque Du Soleil show. "I, uh…" I said as I watched one woman surface from the bottom of the bowl and lick her way up the other's body. "Damn." I scurried away to join the crowd that had gathered around the entertainment.

I maneuvered as close as possible and instantly became one of the silent gawking spectators. The women were gorgeous with their wet white masks and oh-so-tight muscular bodies. They moved with the grace of Olympic gymnasts as they twisted in a multitude of erotic positions that left me in awe.

I definitely need to up my bedroom game.

I watched them lick and suck on each other, until the one woman walked the other to the side of the bowl, turned her around to face the crowd, and pressed her against the bowed glass. The water was only chest deep, so she rested her arms and head on the lip of the bowl, while the other woman began grinding on her backside. Breasts that could rival Ruby the valet's pressed up against the glass, looking like two balloons about to pop. Her moaning may have been a bit over-the-top, but the effect was undeniable. If I thought the women having wall sex was a turn-on, it was nothing compared to this. I shifted my stance, because now my underwear felt like it was completely drenched, and not from the splashing water. My body was on the verge of exploding.

"Fuck." I whispered the word that said it all as the one bowl performer turned the other around, and both walked to the middle of the tank. Water dripped down their exposed upper bodies and snaked around their erect nipples. I nibbled at my lower lip as I leaned toward the bowl, envisioning licking the water off every inch of their way-too-perfect bodies. They stood staring at each other, in all their dripping glory, until the one took a deep breath and dove to the bottom of the bowl. She folded into a handstand, her legs surfacing and gracefully falling on the shoulders of the other, who leaned forward and started licking her clit. A pulse began to beat from between my legs, and I slid my one hand in my front pocket to try to be as discreet as possible while I began touching myself.

"Ah, to be young and limber." A sultry voice startled me and interrupted my concentration.

I glanced at the woman standing next to me, causally sipping on her drink. She had on a black suit that hugged her curves beautifully. Her light gray shirt and matching tie were silky and expensive looking. Her bright red lipstick was a contrast to her plain black mask, and her short, spiky salt-and-pepper hair offset beautiful turquoise eyes. "Your mask is spectacular, by the way," she said as she smiled.

Reluctantly, I turned my full attention to the woman with the sexy voice and exhaled a shaky breath as I tried to calm myself. "Thanks. I, uh…borrowed it from a friend."

"Well, bravo to your friend, because that mask beautifully accents your eyes."

"Thanks," I repeated as I cocked my head toward the woman, whose compliment seemed warm and genuine. "I'm Addison." I pulled my hand from my front pocket and extended it.

"I'm…delighted to meet you. Are you enjoying your evening so far?" she said as she gripped my hand.

"Well, I only got here a few minutes ago." I tried to subtly shift my weight back and forth and redistribute the intense blood flow away from my clit and back to my extremities. "I'm actually looking for Elizabeth Hathaway."

"Isn't everyone." My no-named friend waved her hand as if to brush off the statement as yesterday's news.

"Do you know her?" I said with hope.

"Intimately." She overemphasized the "in" as she said the word.

"Then would you mind pointing her out to me? I'd like to interview her for an article I'm writing for a website I work for."

"An article, how enchanting."

"It would be more enchanting if I could talk with her."

"Well, don't despair, dear, she's around." She gestured to the yard.

"Could you at least tell me what she's wearing? I'd really love to talk with her."

"I could, but where's the fun in that?" The woman smiled and ran a finger under my chin. "Your mask really is spectacular," she said as she sauntered away. "Elizabeth's wearing a black mask, if that helps," she called over her shoulder.

"Yeah, so I've been told," I called back.

I returned my focus to the women in the tank, who were now sensually licking and sucking each other's lips. If the rest of the night was going to be like this, I would be in the bathroom more than once relieving the pressure that was building, and not the one in my bladder. With a heavy sigh, I reminded myself that I really did need to find Elizabeth. I tore myself away from the entertainment and excused myself out of the swelling crowd and decided to check out the body painting tent on the other side of the yard. As I walked back by the pool bar, I asked the bartender if she could pour me a glass of red wine. Any kind of wine was fine with me, I told her. It wasn't about the vintage, blend, or label. At this point, it was about the buzz. A moment later, she handed me a plastic glass and informed me that she chose her favorite. I thanked her and had it half consumed by the time I was at the end of the pool where a group of five people in the Jacuzzi were making out. One lifted her head long enough to call for me to jump in and join them.

I waved her off. I threw out what was now becoming my catchphrase for the evening: "Maybe later." I really needed to stay on task. I shuffled off the pool deck to the far side of the backyard, where a large white tent was set up and a group of people were already gathered around.

I entered the tent, joined the masses, and craned my neck to get a better glimpse of the entertainment. The area accommodated six stations of artists painting naked women of all shapes and sizes with spray guns, traditional brushes, or a combination of both. A line had formed as guests waited their turn, but most, like me, were just there to watch.

I scanned the stations, trying to retain as much detail as possible for my article. In station one, a woman was being transformed into a sunflower. Next to her, another had the pride flag painted around her breast and hip area. The woman in station three looked like a walking Picasso painting, and in station four, a woman's brown skin wielded the beginnings of tiger stripes. But it was station five that really caught my attention. I focused on the tall, stunningly gorgeous woman as she stood seemingly confident in all her naked splendor. Her mask was bright red, her build was athletic, her hair black and long, and I became transfixed as I watched the artist skillfully maneuver a spray gun over her, turning her milky white skin blue, bronze, and burgundy. Her nipples hardened as the spray gun turned on them, and to my disappointment, hid the erect little pink buttons in a layer of burgundy paint. I heard the whispers of those around me guessing as to what the final canvas of her body would reveal, but I intuitively shook my head at all their guesses. I had a hunch she was about to transform into one of my all-time favorite superheroes. And sure enough, twenty minutes later, Wonder Woman stood before us. I wished I had my phone at that moment. We could've doubled our readership with a picture of her alone.

She thanked the artist, then began gracefully strolling in my direction as though she were a model on a runway. Muffled applause and murmurs of approval from the crowd showered her as she displayed her painted body as though it was the must-have fashion for the year. I grabbed another drink off a mobile bar as it wheeled past, downed the wine in three gulps, and hoped it would drown the last of any lingering inhibitions.

"Excuse me," I said as she approached. "Could I, um… would you mind if I ask you a few questions?" For the sake of my article, and maybe my fantasies, I wanted to know what it was like to get body-painted, without actually doing it.

She hesitated, gave me the once-over, then smiled. "Sure." She cocked her hip and stood relaxed.

I closed the distance between us. "What did it feel like getting your body painted?"

"It turned me on."

I was hoping for a little more detail, but when none was forthcoming, I nudged the conversation a bit. "In what way?"

She bent forward until her lips tickled my ear. "Like the air coming out of the spray gun was a woman tending to every inch of my body with her warm breath, except for one little area that for obvious reasons still needs tending to. If you're interested in helping with that, all you'd have to do is pucker your lips and blow." She leaned back and winked. "I'm going for a drink at the jellyfish bar. Come find me," she said as she sauntered away.

I puckered my lips and blew out a soft whistle. She paused, twisted her upper body toward me, and cocked her head. "I was just practicing blowing," I explained through a smile.

She laughed, then turned toward the house, and I watched every step that wonder of a woman took. I wanted to follow her serenade. The lure of her call was enticing, but instead, I stayed rooted in the tent. A Sandy devil popped up on my left shoulder and began nudging me. "Go on, what are you waiting for? This is why you're here. It's a sex party, for fuck's sake, go have some sex."

I nodded and took a step forward as a Michelle devil popped up on my opposite shoulder and poked her little red trident into my neck. Or was that a mosquito bite? I slapped at my neck either way. "You are here for one reason only. Get me that exclusive interview with Elizabeth. You have one shot at this, don't blow it!"

"She wears the outfit well, wouldn't you say?" The familiar sultry voice broke my devil debate as the internal voices of Sandy and Michelle evaporated.

"Yeah," I said as I glanced at the woman I met at the water bowl through the corner of my eye, the two of us craning our necks as we watched Wonder Woman round the corner and meander inside.

"You should follow her. She seemed very interested in you."

"You think so?" It's true, the Sandy devil was winning, and as thoughts of sex with the body-painted goddess danced in my head, I took another step in her direction.

"Oh please...she couldn't have spelled it out any clearer. Go...enjoy. After all, isn't that why you're here?"

Is it, though? I shook off the lustful thoughts and calmed my throbbing clit. First the interview, then the entertainment, I reminded myself. "I actually really need to track down Elizabeth Hathaway."

"You would rather pass on that magnificent specimen to talk with that old coot?"

When she put it like that, it did cause me a moment of pause. "Yeah." I quickly shifted back into business mode. "It would really help me a lot if I could just have a moment of her time."

"It means that much to you to talk with Elizabeth?"

I nodded. "It does."

"Well." She sized me up, then hooked her arm around mine. "If you honestly think that's more important than sex, then let's go find her, shall we? It'll be like our own little scavenger hunt. And this way, it'll give us a chance to get to know one another better," she said as she gently patted my forearm.

And just like that, I was whisked away back into the mansion. If our hunt ended in success, I was on my way to snagging the story that would propel our website's readership, and hopefully my career, to a pivotal level.

I followed along as my escort guided me through various parts of the estate. We stopped periodically when she thought she saw Elizabeth, but just as quickly we were back in motion when upon further inspection she announced, "Nope, that's not her."

As we fluttered around, I took the opportunity to pepper her with questions. How did she know Elizabeth? Was this her first time at the ball? Did she know the story behind what prompted Elizabeth to have an annual sex party? But instead of giving me details, she gave vague, generic, and incomplete answers to all my questions, as the distractions of the event and its guests seemed more enticing to her than my inquiries. It was like trying to get the full attention of a five-year-old in a candy store.

"Well," she said as we finally paused for a long moment. "Since she's not around the main area, she must be in one of the rooms." And off we went down a long hallway that seemed to go on forever. I tried again to strike up a conversation about Elizabeth, but she skillfully turned the tables on me and began asking questions about my life. What brought me to Vegas? Did I enjoy being a reporter? What were my aspirations? But unlike her, I enthusiastically answered each one in animated detail, as though I was once again a kid coming home and telling my mom every single detail that happened at school that day. My escort nodded and smiled as she let me babble on, until we finally stopped our motion outside the door with a sign on an easel that designated it as the game room. She held up a finger signaling that my monologuing needed to pause as she gently cracked opened the door and I craned my neck around her. The room had several green felt tables scattered around, and it was clear the only game being played in this space was strip poker. Several of the staff and guests paused for a moment as they looked up and nodded toward us.

"Hope everyone's having fun. Sorry for the interruption. Carry on. Hmm." She turned to me as she closed the door. "I didn't see her in there either."

The theater, gym, and bowling alley were also a bust as far as finding Elizabeth. "Looks like the old broad is harder to find than a cockroach in a kitchen." She laughed at her own joke as her smooth, deep voice cackled a bit. It was then that I decided to name her after my favorite oldies but goodies sultry-voiced actress, Lauren Bacall.

We circled back to the main room and finally came to rest at the far corner by the kitchen. "Ah." She snapped her fingers. "I know where she might be. Follow me," Lauren announced as she grabbed a tray of chocolate-covered strawberries off a mobile cart as it wheeled by and guided me over to a set of closed doors.

"Hit that button, won't you, darling." She motioned with a nod. "The one to the right of the doors."

I turned and looked at a wall covered in a beautiful subtle wallpaper whose fabric mimicked the outer bark of a birch tree. "I don't see a button," I said as I leaned in and squinted.

"Rub your hand down the wall, close to the door. You'll find it."

I did as she said, and sure enough, there was a button so discreetly blended into the design of the wallpaper I would have never known it was there. I pressed it, and the faux doors immediately slid sideways, exposing an elevator car.

"A private elevator." I chuckled as we stepped in. "But of course."

"Why take the stairs, darling, when you can fly!" She cackled as the doors closed.

I stepped to the back of the car, leaned against the far wall, and took the opportunity to really look Lauren over. Even with her mask on, I could tell many things about this woman. She moved with the grace of a queen, seemed to possess a strong self-confidence, and the designer label on her clothes told me they were well above my pay grade. The deep-set lines around her lips and eyes and the spots on her tan wrinkled hands told me she had traveled many times around the sun, making memories on this planet long before I was even born. And yet, as our eyes locked and she turned the tips of her lips up, I didn't focus on the obvious age or economic gap between us. Instead, all I could see in that moment was someone who I was becoming enchanted with. Someone who was articulate, witty, sophisticated, and polite. Not to mention that sexy, sultry, "come fuck me" voice that was starting to make my knees buckle a bit.

The settling of the elevator made me turn and face the opening doors. "Holy shit," I said as I stepped into a dimly lit bedroom with at least two dozen flameless candles flickering, adding to the ambience of a space that was at least four times the size of my entire apartment. A king-sized canopied bed was against the wall to my left, flanked by a full sitting area on one side and a massage table and two zero gravity massage chairs on the other.

Lauren stepped around me and placed the tray of fruit on a small round table in the sitting area as I continued to spin in a circle. On the opposite wall from the bed was a stone fireplace that seemed tall enough for me to stand in. Floor-to-ceiling windows were on either side of the fireplace, and I walked over and stood in awe as I gazed out at the most magnificent view of the Strip I had ever seen. We were at the right distance and height to see the entire display of all its twinkling splendor.

"Wow," I said as I momentarily glanced at Lauren, who stood off to my side, her arms folded across her chest. "With a view like this, I don't think I would ever want to leave this room."

"It is a rather mesmerizing display of neon, isn't it?" she said before we both fell into a comfortable silence.

After a long moment, I turned my attention back to her. "This is Elizabeth's bedroom, isn't it?"

She nodded. "It is."

"Won't we get in trouble being in here?" I remembered the stern warning from Shelly about this room being off-limits.

"Tell me something, Addison, haven't you ever done something in your life that you knew you shouldn't, but you did it anyway because the thrill of doing it outweighed the consequences?"

I hesitated before answering as I reflected on an early life lesson my rather abusive father taught me about the consequences of what happened when I didn't follow the rules. Because of that, I had, for the most part, always stayed in my lane of life and didn't deviate much from what was expected of me, and I rarely, if ever, bucked the system. "We should probably get going. I really don't think it's a good idea that—"

"Shh."

Her finger pressed against my lips, silencing me. "Let's not think about what we shouldn't be doing, and instead think about what we *could* be doing." Lauren extended her hand. "Let's have a little fun, shall we?"

I rested my fingers on hers for a moment before she squeezed and took control. She led me into a bathroom about half the size of the master suite. I'm sure it had all the necessary amenities a bathroom had—toilet, closet, sink, and drawers—but I didn't notice, because I was focused on the small swimming pool encased in marble that sat in the corner of the room. "Don't tell me that's a bathtub?" I snorted, because I had never seen a tub big enough to easily fit a dozen people in it with plenty of elbow room.

Lauren moved around me. "Oh, it's more than a bathtub," she said as she hit one of two buttons by the three steps leading up to the tub. The water immediately churned as bubbles formed at the surface. "Tell me something, Addison, have you ever made love in a Jacuzzi?"

My stomach did a flip-flop as the question hit me between the legs. This was no longer about finding Elizabeth. "Um, no, I, uh, haven't."

She circled me, then leaned in and whispered in my ear. "You'd be amazed at how a jet placed in the right spot between your legs feels like a dozen tongues licking you at the same time." She kissed the words down my neck.

I leaned my head back to give her more skin, as I imagined the feeling of a dozen tongues licking me. "I...um, I really do need to find Elizabeth." I leaned forward and tried to break the spell she was placing on me.

"Who you need to find is yourself. Tonight is about letting go...about not having a predetermined agenda," she said in her low, sultry voice as she reached from behind me and began unbuttoning my shirt. "It's about finding that place inside you that can take you to levels you've never reached. It's about growing the woman within." She made the statement as she finished her task, and a slight chill tickled its way up my exposed skin.

I stood paralyzed, wanting and waiting for her next move.

"Lick my fingers," she said as she brought her right hand up to my lips. I bent forward and sucked them into my mouth. She moaned. We stayed like that for a moment, until she gently pulled her fingers away from my tongue and slid them under my dangling shirt. The wetness found my nipple, and she pinched and played in that space until I told her with my accelerated breath that I was desiring more.

"Not yet," she whispered as though she read my mind. She seemed confident in what she was doing, and I intuitively knew if I gave myself to her, I'd be in experienced hands.

Another pinch to my nipple caused me to catch my breath. The pressure was just on the verge of pain yet was somehow extremely pleasing. The wetness between my legs released, as though that nipple was the switch to a faucet that was now on steady flow.

"Earlier, you asked me what the meaning of this ball was all about…" Lauren began unbuckling my belt with her right hand. "The answer to that question lies within you. Tell me, Addison, what does it mean to you to have the ability and freedom to completely express yourself?" She began rubbing the fingers of her other hand through my hair, and I fell deeper into her trance. "To unlock all of the fantasies that you hold up here," she asked as she pushed her fingers deeper into my scalp. "And let them play out down here…" She slid her other hand down my pants and cupped me between my legs.

I stood speechless, unable to answer as I leaned back into her. She had me, and she knew it.

"I'm going to get undressed now, and I want you to do the same." She moved away from me, and we both began disrobing, neither taking our eyes off the other. Her body was a little curvy, her breasts were average, and her nipples perky and pink. She was beautiful and I couldn't wait to give myself over to her.

I stepped out of my clothes and stood at the edge of the tub. A shiver went through me. Not because I was cold, but because I was finding it harder and harder to refrain from turning to her and telling her to hurry up and fuck me already.

"Patience," she said, and I wondered again if she had an uncanny way of reading my mind. I let out a shaky breath as we both stood in our nakedness, our masks the only thing still covering a part of our flesh. I reached up to remove mine and she stopped me.

"Leave it on. That's the rules of the masquerade. Your identity is not relevant here. Tonight is not about who you are, or what your title is…it's about how you feel. Anonymity can be a powerful thing, my dear. Lack of identity brings lack of inhibitions," she said as she extended her hand and led me up the marble steps and then down the descending three. We stood for a moment in the warm water before she released my hand and shuffled to the far side of the Jacuzzi. She sat down, chest deep in the water, rested her arms on the ledge, leaned her head back, and closed her eyes. The bubbles swirled around the tips of her breasts, lapping around them in a way that I wished my tongue was doing.

"Tonight," she said, "wealth, power, title, or degree don't matter. We're all here equally, playing in the shadows, behind a cloak of freedom from the face we must wear for the rest of the world. Tonight is about the inner Addison that has yet to show herself, because up until now, she hasn't allowed that side of her to come out and play."

I stared at this woman who seemed to read me as easily as an open book. Had I ever truly opened up and allowed myself to express the inner urges I fantasized about while I pleasured myself? To know what it would be like to have those thoughts played out in real time? I had only been with four women in my life, and while each was wonderful, all had a traditional and conservative side when it came to sex.

"Tell me something, Addison..." She brought her hands down and rubbed them around her breasts. "When was the last time you gave yourself over to someone and sat back and truly enjoyed the ride? Hmm?" I could tell even with her mask on that she arched a brow, as she settled lower in the water, resting her head back and closed her eyes.

So that was it, I thought as I stood watching her. She had cast the lure with her words, and now she sat back and seemed to confidently wait for me to take the bait. I wondered if she could sense my hesitancy and inner dialogue. Who was this sultry-voiced woman? My gut said it was Elizabeth, but I had no evidence to back it. But did it really matter who she was? No. She was right. Tonight was not about formalities or identities. Tonight was about one thing. The question was, could I get out of my head long enough to just...be?

In the end, she didn't have to reel me in, I came willingly, as I sensed she knew I would. And as I approached and stood over her, a slight smile appeared on her face as her crystal-clear turquoise eyes presented themselves under her mask.

"I, um...I don't know what to say," I said, and yet deep down

I wanted to say so much. I wanted to tell her all the things I've always wanted to try with a lover, and equally as many things I wanted to feel.

"Then don't say anything. Talk to me in another way. A way that we both understand. A way that says a woman knows what to give another woman, because she knows exactly how it feels when she's on the receiving end. Everything I am about to do to you, I can honestly say I know how it feels." She stood and tapped my head. "Remember, you need to separate your mind from your..." She trailed her finger down past my heart until it rested just outside my clit, where she began playing in my wetness. I let out a breath as my stomach lurched. "You see, darling, I know exactly what you're feeling right now and what you want. The only thing you need to tell me is how hard you like it. And I have confidence you'll find a way to let me know."

That was all it took for me to push my mental poker chips forward, because holy fuck, I was all in at this point. I bent forward and kissed her. Our tongues danced around each other in perfect synchronicity as they made the official introduction between us before she took over and began kissing me hard and long. It was a prelude to the way I knew she would take me.

"Turn around," she said, her breathing heavy from our kiss.

She spun me around before my mind could even process what she was asking of me. "Position yourself in the area between the seats, spread your legs, and inch closer to the side of the tub." She reached around me and twisted one of the jet nozzles so instead of spraying the water forward, it sprayed it up.

"The jets in this tub are all customized." With her one hand on my back, she guided me forward. "Take another step and lean over and you'll understand. And I suggest you ease into it."

I did as she instructed, and as soon as the spray of water hit my clit, I jumped back. I knew I would like this, but I wasn't prepared for such an intense feeling.

"Ease into it," she repeated as she pressed her body against mine, fusing our skin together. "I want to feel you move on it."

I nodded and slowly inched forward as she mimicked my every move, never letting space come between us. I felt the swooshing of water and bubbles tickle my clit. I caught my breath. It was like having a vibrating wand on high pulsing me, and at first the pressure was still too intense, as I tried again to back off, but I could feel Lauren's body stiffen and stop my retreat.

"Don't resist it. Let your body appreciate the intensity and take deep breaths. You will find it is a sensation that you will soon crave. Desire the intensity. Don't resist it," she repeated as she tickled the words on my neck as she bent me forward. I reached out with locked arms to balance myself on the edge of the tub. I spread my legs a little wider over the stream of the water and took a deep breath, then two, as I tried to relax my muscles. I felt Lauren's body pressed firmly against my back and butt. She brought her hands, full of water, up and cupped my dangling breasts. Her hands were warm and wet as her fingers caressed and massaged me. I closed my eyes and tried to focus, but my mind was split with the sensation of the jet stroking my clit as much as her hands were stroking my breasts. It was like a battle of my body over which stimulation would win my attention when my eyes flew open. The pinch to my nipples wasn't a painful one, but like the jet, it was intense, and as she rolled the tips of my breasts between her fingers, I had to clear my head and do as she said. I took a deep breath, tensed ever so slightly as the water danced between my legs and tickled my clit, and gave myself over to this new sensation.

"What do you feel?" Lauren said, her breath warm on my neck.

I closed my eyes and concentrated. "I feel…" I moaned. "Like I'm about to come," I said as I moved my body in small circles over the jet.

"But what does coming feel like?" she said as she maintained her pressure against my back.

"Like…like…" I took another deep breath as I refocused on my body. I wanted to conjure up my go-to *come fantasy* about being fucked by my favorite Hollywood actress in her trailer while on the set of her latest action film. But what Lauren had said earlier stuck in my mind. This experience was about me finding myself, and to do that, I had to stay in the moment. I had to stay with *me*, and not float away into a scripted and very overplayed fantasy.

"What do you feel?" she asked again.

I stilled my mind and listened to my body. "Like the blood is rushing to my clit, and it's causing my muscles to strain because…because…"

"Yes…that's it…tell me why your muscles are straining. What do they want right now? What do you want right now?"

As much as the stimulation of the water had me teetering on the edge of the cliff, I knew it alone couldn't get me there, and I knew what it would take to make me explode. "I want to be penetrated," I said.

"With what? What exactly do you want me to penetrate you with?"

At that point, I really didn't care, as long as it would fill me up and go deep. Three fingers, a dildo, anything just to push me off this cliff that I was precariously dangling from. I felt her one hand release from my nipple and slowly trickle down my body. She ran it up and down my clit, stopping and barely going in with the tip of her finger when she reached the opening. She was teasing me, and it was driving me nuts.

"Do you want this?" she said as her fingers perched at my opening.

I nodded and moaned.

"I'm sorry, I didn't hear you."

"Yes," I whispered through a strained jaw. "You know I do."

"Then close your eyes and bend over further. And don't you dare come until I say so."

I closed my eyes and leaned forward, which meant I was off the jet spray. I felt her slide down my back and her arm reach between my legs, and at first, I thought she wanted me to hump her forearm, but I soon realized she was reaching for the jet. I heard a soft grunt.

"Tell me when the water is in the right position for you," she said. "The jet is completely adjustable."

I nodded as I felt the bubbles, those stimulating and intoxicating tongues come closer...closer...closer... I tensed. "There," I said as I flexed my thighs and exhaled a breath. I felt her wet warm body fuse once again with mine as she bent over me.

"I am going to give you what you want, and in turn, you are going to give me what I want." She licked her tongue up my ear for added delight. I shivered.

"What, um..." I could barely form words, much less a sentence. "What do you want?"

"I want you to show me who you really are. I want to see you let loose and let your inner desires dictate this dance. Do you understand?"

I nodded.

"I still can't hear you."

"I understand." I heard my words come from a faraway place as a desperation came over me. I really needed to release.

"Good, then I will give you what you want."

She peeled her warm, wet upper body off mine. I could feel the temperature drop as air moved into the space where there was none before. Her soft wet tongue started at the base of my neck and sucked and licked its way to where the water's edge was, then back up. I tilted my head from shoulder to shoulder. The ache returned and the intensity of the jet told me I needed to come soon, or I would be too overstimulated. Lauren must have sensed this because she stood, her thighs pressed firmly against my ass. And a moment later, I felt her warm hand return to my nipples. And just like before, she pinched and rolled them between her fingers, with grace and ease. She used the right amount of pressure as she played rough at first, then backed off enough and administered a soft gentleness that made me want the roughness to return. She took her right hand out of the water and ran it down my back until it broke the surface of the water as it tickled its way down my ass and came to a rest between my legs.

"I'm going to fuck you now, but think of it more as though you are pleasuring yourself. I'll give you the means that'll make you come, but you dictate the pace."

At this point, I didn't bother to nod or answer. I just wanted to release the buildup. Her one hand maintained pinching my nipple while the fingers from her other tickled my clit, as though she were strumming a harp. I could feel each fingertip move up and down my wetness independently of the others, until as if on cue, they all came together as one. They were right there, as if waiting for me to sink lower in the water and escort them into me. Was that what she wanted? For me to make the next move? We were both still, except for her left hand, which continued to roll my nipple between her fingers.

"Tell me what you want?" she whispered, and once again her voice sounded like a distant serenade.

"I want you to fuck me," I said, because doesn't that one word say it all?

"Darling, the word 'fuck' isn't always definitive, so you'll have to tell me exactly what that means. Tell me in detail. Describe it to me. Tell me how you want me to please you," she said as the tips of her fingers entered me, then paused. "Is this what you want?"

"Yes," I moaned.

She pushed her fingers in a little deeper, but just barely.

"How about this?" she said as she leaned over me.

I nodded.

"Then talk to me…tell me in your words what it is that 'fuck' means to you."

I was going crazy at this point. The water from the jet was

holding my clit hostage as it sprayed, and her fingers were on the verge of penetrating and fulfilling my desire, and she was asking me to not only talk but to express words that could form complete sentences. "Fuck," I said out of frustration because at that point, all I wanted to do was escape in my mind and get off. I exhaled, then nodded. The only way I was going to get what I wanted was to stay in the present and play her game. "I want to feel the flesh of your fingers stroke the inside of me."

"Flesh on flesh," she added. "The dance of lovemaking."

"Yes, and I want to feel you move deep inside me. Like you're taking every inch of me, leaving nothing left untouched, as you work your way closer to the spot that you know will make me come."

"And where is that spot?" she hissed on my neck.

"You'll know it because I'll tell you."

"That's right, remember, you dictate this dance," she whispered again as she moved her fingers in and out but wasn't giving me the depth I wanted. I finally took charge and lowered myself on her hand, letting myself swallow her fingers. I moved up and down, harder and faster, as I felt her fingers fill me up. The jet was spraying on my front and her fingers were stroking me on the inside. I could hear the water began to splash around me as I moved faster and faster on her hand. She pinched my nipple harder, and the sensation was surprisingly exciting. The build was coming; I could feel my body get ready. I strained my thighs, and my stomach muscles followed suit as I pressed my body deeper on her fingers. There wasn't an inch of me that wasn't being fucked right now.

"Yes, darling." She bent and whispered in my ear. "You can come now."

I exploded with convulsions as a moan escaped my throat that I had never heard before. I continued to move fast and hard on her fingers until the pulsing on the inside matched the intensity of the jets. I soon slowed my motion and let the twitching play out until I needed… "Pressure," I moaned. "I need pressure," I repeated as I moved off her fingers.

She understood, of course she did, she was a woman, so she knew exactly what I was feeling. She cupped her hand and pressed it over my clit. I settled my weight on her arm and hand, then rocked a bit, until the last of the orgasm subsided. I arched my back as my body went limp. She embraced me, then turned me around to face her. Lauren's turquoise eyes sparkled from behind her mask as she stared at me, her lips once again turning up at the edges.

"There now, so much better than the all-serious person you were when you first got here."

I felt my cheeks flush with embarrassed heat, and I bowed my head until her finger tipped the edge of my chin up. We locked eyes. I was still in the aftermath of an orgasm that was more intense than any I had had to date. "I, um, thank you, that was…" I paused, searching for the right word to fully express what she had given me, but she placed one finger across my lips to silence me yet again.

"Oh, darling, if you think for one moment that we're done, you are sorely mistaken. Fucking was never meant to be a one-off. The night is still young. But for now, let's grab a nibble and take a breath, shall we?"

Lauren turned and exited the Jacuzzi with grace as water dripped and snaked its way down her body, leaving a trail of small puddles in her wake. "Be right back," she said as she strolled to the closet, grabbed a plush white robe, shrugged it on, then headed into the other room.

I settled into one of the seats, leaned back, and let my body relax under the warmth of the of the water. I closed my eyes, cleared my mind, and thought life didn't get much better than this.

"Ready for a post-orgasmic treat?" she announced as she reentered the bathroom.

I peeled my eyes opened and chuckled as Lauren stood in the doorway posing with one hand on her hip and the other under a tray of chocolate-covered strawberries held high. "Care to join?" she said with a tilt of her head as she ambled to one of two oversized chaise lounge chairs that sat in the opposite corner of the bathroom and placed the tray on a small table between the furniture.

"I'd love to." I waded over to the steps and ambled out of the Jacuzzi. Lauren scurried over to the closet, grabbed a second robe, and met me at the base of the tub, where my feet were encased with memory foam softness from the bath rug. I wiggled my toes and made a mental note to myself that I needed to get one of these to put outside my shower, because holy hell... "This rug feels amazing. I wonder if they make insoles out of this material?" I said as Lauren opened the robe for me. I hesitated. "Do you think that's a good idea? I mean, what if Elizabeth—"

"I won't tell if you don't," she interrupted as she wrapped the plush material around me, extended a hand, and led me over to the chairs.

"Is this..." I let my thoughts trail off as I rubbed my fingers down the textured pink Himalayan colored walls, then brought them to my lips for a taste.

"Salt? Yes, it is," she said as she flipped a switch activating a heat lamp set in the ceiling directly above the chairs. "They say it's supposed to be beneficial to your health and all that guru rigamarole, but who the hell knows. I do, however, think it's a divine shade of pink, don't you?"

I nodded, because even though pink was my least favorite color, I had to admit, the walls did look pretty cool with a layer of salt on them.

"Come. Sit," she said as she grabbed a chocolate-covered strawberry and slid into one of the chaise lounges that seemed a bit excessive and bulky. But what in this house wasn't over-the-top in size and scale?

"Mmm." Lauren bit into the candy-covered fruit and moaned as a trickle of juice from the berry dripped down her chin. "These are delish. You have to have one."

"Don't mind if I do," I said as I flopped into the chair beside her. The fabric that encased my body was as soft as the rug.

"There are buttons on the side of the chair that control the tilt for your back and legs," she instructed as she pointed.

I began pressing the controls, and the chair responded by tilting my upper body back and lifting my legs, up and down, until I found the perfect combination and angle.

"You good?" Lauren said with an amused tone to her voice as she turned her head toward me.

"Yes, I'm good. Thank you," I replied in a moment of indulgent bliss.

"Now then, care for a strawberry?"

As a matter of fact, I was feeling a little hungry from skipping dinner so I could make it to the party on time, and I suddenly felt as though I could devour every berry on the tray in a hedonistic display of hunger. Instead, I politely reached for the largest one, but Lauren placed her hand over mine, stopping my motion.

"Please, allow me," she said as she pinched the green stem and dangled the fruit from her fingers.

She slowly peeled herself from her chair, kneeled beside me, parted my robe, cocked her leg, and straddled me as she lowered her clit onto my stomach. I could feel her wetness as she took the moment to settle herself on my abs. When she seemed content, she smiled that sexy smile as she tilted her head, and I knew she was sizing me up like a painter would a blank canvas.

"What?" I said because I wanted to know what I was in for.

"I think," she said as she trailed the tips of the fingers of one hand over my breasts, "it's time for a little indulgence."

The moment she finished her sentence, she placed the stem of the strawberry between her teeth and slowly leaned forward. I parted my lips anticipating the delicious sweetness of the chocolate-dipped fruit, and as soon as I felt the tip of the strawberry inserted into my mouth, I closed my eyes and ran my tongue over the smooth creaminess of the berry's bottom. As the layer of chocolate melted on my tongue, I picked up hints of brandy mixed into the sugary goodness. I moaned at the pairing of flavors.

Lauren pressed the fruit further into my mouth, and I spread my lips, graciously accepting the entire strawberry. When she stopped her motion, our lips were barely touching, and I could feel her breath on my face as she paused as though she were waiting for me to make the next move.

I bit down, and an explosion of juicy sweet and semi-bitter flavors filled my mouth as I chewed. With a quick cock of her head, she spit the stem out and returned her lips to mine. At first she seemed content to linger in that position, letting my lips glide over hers as I chewed on the fruit. But I could sense she wanted more.

The moment I swallowed, she thrust her tongue into my mouth and searched for mine. I greeted hers and wondered if the moan she emitted was from the lingering flavors that were remaining on my tongue, or what was yet to come. We stayed in our dance of hunger, devouring each other until she leaned out of the kiss and settled her hips back around my waist.

"I want the rest of you to taste as delicious as your mouth does." She pulled the sash from her robe. "Wrists, please." She motioned with a nod.

I presented my hands as though they were about to be cuffed.

"Let me know if it's too tight," she said as she wrapped one end of the sash around my wrists in a figure eight, knotted it, then gently guided my arms over my head. She pressed the controls on the chair until it reclined to a level position, leaned over me, and hooked the other end of the sash on what looked like a towel rack attached to the wall. I wiggled my wrist just enough to test the effectiveness of Lauren's knot, and let's just say she would never make a decent sailor.

"Comfy?" she asked as she snagged two strawberries off the tray.

"I am," I reassured her. In fact, with the warmth of the lamps, the slight aroma emitting from the salt, the taste of the chocolate-covered strawberry still lingering on my lips, and the plush robe around my body, I could honestly say the conditions reminded me of an overpriced day at one of the casino spas. Minus, of course, the fact that my arms were bound, a naked woman was straddling me, and I'd just been fucked three ways from Sunday in a Jacuzzi, the similarities were strikingly similar.

"Good. Then let's begin, shall we?" She placed the bottom of the strawberries on my stomach and slowly began moving them over my upper body in a haphazard pattern. At first, it tickled a bit as the slightly cooler chocolate made contact with the warmth of my skin, but the candy quickly warmed and as I craned my neck and glanced at the serious expression on Lauren's face, I knew she was creating a chocolatey masterpiece on my flesh. I thought about the body-spraying tent and what the woman told me about the sensation of touch on her skin, and I thought, if being painted with a chocolate-covered strawberry felt this pleasant, I could only image what it felt like having your entire body tended to.

When Lauren was done with the strawberries in hand, she discarded them on the tray and grabbed two more. She repeated this motion until she finally declared herself done. With a satisfied tilt to her head, she took a moment to study her creation. The gleam in her eyes told me she was pleased with her artwork.

"Now then," she said as she plucked the stems off two new berries and held one to my lips. "Be a dear and bite this in half."

I gladly did as I was told.

"And this one too," she said as she held the other strawberry to my mouth.

I bit into the delicious goodness. Maybe it was the setting, or the fact that I really was hungrier than I thought, but those strawberries were the best I've ever tasted. I closed my eyes, savoring every bite, and as soon as I swallowed, I felt something

• 216 •

soft and wet squish onto my nipples. I craned my neck, glanced over my body, and chuckled at what I saw. The upper half of the strawberries covered both of my breasts.

"You look delicious enough to eat. In fact," she said. "I think I will."

I lowered my head back onto the cushion because I knew, as I felt Lauren reposition her body a little lower on mine, that I was about to take another incredible ride on her fantasy train.

"Close your eyes," she whispered. "And tap your senses. I want you to feel my tongue mix with the juices and sweetness on your body until I lick every drop of wetness from your flesh."

My body shivered as though a blast of arctic air blew tiny icicles over my skin, and as per her request, I closed my eyelids to the surrounding room and let the sensation of touch tell the story of what she was about to do to me. I lay in my own darkness and imagination as I waited for the entertainment to begin.

I didn't have to wait long before I felt her warm, moist tongue introduce itself to my belly button, then settle deeper into my flesh as it began circling the vicinity. Her soft lips joined in as she began sucking and licking her way around my abdomen. I imagined her wet mouth following every inch and turn of the sugary path she had laid out moments before.

Lauren took her time climbing my body, lingering in some areas longer than others, and for whatever reason, at those locations, she sucked a little harder. The wetness between my legs reemerged and my body, although a comfortable temperature from the heat lamps, tingled as the warm breath from her nostrils floated across my skin.

She soon settled in the area just under my breast, and as she began slowly sucking her way up my B-cup flesh, my nipples hardened under the berry because I knew they were next on her menu. I tried to scoot my body down as I wordlessly conveyed that I wanted—no, desired her lips to suck my nipples, but she tortured me with time as she played with my breasts first before accommodating my request.

The moment she inserted the strawberry in her mouth, I arched my back and moaned. Between the explosion of extra juiciness from the fruit and the sensation of her tongue dancing between the berry and my nipple, I was about to come. And every time she let her teeth gently bite down into my flesh, it sent another arctic chill through my body. Fuck, I really wanted her inside me.

"I, uh, want you to..." I barely said the beginning of my desire when once again her finger rested against my lips, silencing me.

"Shh. Your role in this ride is to feel, not speak."

I sucked her finger into my mouth, acknowledging her demand and hopefully conveying a message at the same time. She moved her finger in and out as she finished with my one breast, licking the last of the sticky wetness off my nipple before proceeding to its sister. She attacked the second strawberry with the same hunger, taking my breast along for the stimulating ride. The texture of her tongue and the flesh of the berry melded as one. And as with the other, she seemed to take her time devouring the fruit, making sure every drop of the red juicy evidence was licked from the scene.

She retracted her finger from my mouth and slithered it down my stomach until it met my wetness. "Someone's excited to see me." She chuckled in her sultry cackly voice, and I heard another strawberry being plucked from the tray.

"Do me a favor, darling, and suck the chocolate off this magnificent fruit, would you? But don't bite it."

I parted my lips as a strawberry laced in goodness was placed in my mouth. I wrapped my tongue around the coating and felt the chocolate release its grip on the berry and melt into my mouth. When the smoothness of the candy was replaced with the seedy textured surface of the fruit, I nodded to Lauren. She pulled the strawberry out of my mouth and began kissing her way down my body until she settled between my legs.

By this point, I just wanted her to fuck me like she had in the

Jacuzzi. Hard and deep and relieve the ache that she knew she had created. I spread my legs wider to accommodate her and silently thanked Elizabeth Hathaway for her opulent taste in oversized and grandiose furniture, which was now accommodating us quite nicely.

Lauren readjusted herself, and all my senses became on heightened alert. I was about to be the recipient of some yet undetermined sex act with a strawberry, and as my mind began racing with the many possibilities, the answer presented itself.

A rush of cool juiciness mixed with my own wetness, and I knew that she had squeezed the berry's flesh over my clit, but I didn't know if the liquid now dripping between my legs was more mine or the strawberry's. Before I could ruminate on that thought any further, Lauren's tongue skillfully moved in circles as her lips sucked the wetness from my inner thighs, coming close, so fucking close, to my clit. I squirmed and moved in her direction because I wanted her mouth on my sweet spot. But Lauren made sure no matter how much I begged, she kept her mouth just out of reach. She would lick my clit when she wanted, not when I wanted. A reminder: I was not in control of this ride, she was.

I exhaled a long breath acknowledging my surrender and concentrated on what I was in control of. I focused again on the way her tongue effortlessly moved over my skin, the warmth of her breath, and the tip of her finger, now between my legs, that was picking up speed as it flicked up and down my slickness. I tightened my thigh muscles and arched my back as I focused on the motion of her finger and the pacing of her strokes until I couldn't take it any longer. As soon as I felt her finger slide down, I pushed myself onto her. "Yes, baby." I said the universal words that conveyed that this was what I wanted, even though I knew she was not mine to call *baby*. But at this point I didn't really give a fuck, because all I wanted was to *be* fucked…again.

I rocked my hips and settled myself deeper on her as she thrust in and out, pressing her finger hard against the inside of me so I could feel every inch of her movement. I squeezed around her finger, holding it as I did when it was inside my mouth, as she continued stroking me.

I wanted to rise up on my elbows and use the leverage of the position to push even deeper onto her finger, but the sash reminded me that my hands were still bound, and for now, I needed to rely on Lauren to provide the needed depth. As if on cue, she thrust her finger deeper inside me and pressed her lips on my clit. And just as she had with my nipples, she began sucking and licking the area. I moved on her, driving my body deeper into her, and she responded by sucking even harder…faster…harder. Yeah…right there…right…and just as I felt my body begin its ascent into its release, she shoved two more fingers in, and that gave me the wind I needed to take flight. I rocked my body wildly to the beat of the pulsing as she continued to fuck and suck me.

I wanted to hold on to this feeling, this moment when the world stilled and nothing else seemed to matter. But like always, my flight into ecstasy never lasted as long as I'd like it to, and soon, my body began to calm. Lauren seemed to sense this and slowly pulled her fingers out but maintained the pressure on my clit with her mouth. Eventually, my heart rate and breathing slowed and I became aware that beads of sweat were pooling on my skin.

What the actual fuck, I thought, almost stunned by how my body had responded to this woman's touch. Back-to-back orgasms was not what I was known for, or capable of…or so I thought.

She gave one last lick to my clit before she cat-crawled her way up my body. She stayed on all fours as she leaned over me, trying to untie the sash that held my arms, but in the excitement, I must have pulled the knot tighter, because I could tell by her groans that she was struggling with it.

"Oh, for fuck's sake," she grumbled as she rolled off the lounge chair and stood over me. At that angle, she easily loosened the sash enough for me to slip my hands free.

I pushed a button on the chair and raised the back as Lauren grabbed the tray of strawberries.

"Whaddaya say we go into the other room and finish off these treats," she said with a tilt of her head. "I don't know about you, but I'm feeling a little parched."

I closed my robe, swung my legs off the chair, and followed behind as she led me into the main part of the bedroom. We shuffled over to the massage table, and she motioned with two quick pats to the padding for me to hop up. I did, and as she placed the tray beside me, I grabbed a strawberry and plopped it into my mouth. Another two followed right behind that one. Lauren smiled, grabbed one for herself, and sashayed over to a huge armoire.

"What's your favorite color?" she called over her shoulder as she opened two huge antique-looking wooden doors.

"Um...blue," I answered as I licked the recently dripped juice off my fingers, craned my neck, and squinted in her direction. The room was too dim to completely make out the variety of items dangling from the walls of the armoire, but I had a pretty good guess what type of sexual fantasies those items could accommodate.

"Blue is a rather magnificent color, isn't it," she said as she bent forward and began rummaging through some items. "Now where did I...ah!" She turned with box in hand, ripped it open, and pulled out a blue speckled dildo. "And blue with a flash of color is even better, don't you think?"

I laughed. "Yes, it is," I said and wondered if I had said green, would she have been able to pull one out of her magic chest as well.

"I picked the size that's about three fingers thick, since you seemed to rather enjoy that," Lauren said as she unhooked a black leather strap hanging from the wall of the armoire.

My eyes darted between the dildo and the strap-on as the wetness returned between my legs, and I wondered at this rate how many more strawberries I would have to eat to ward off dehydration.

Lauren approached and stood in front of me. "Hmm, I'm sensing something from you. Do you not like dildos?"

"I do, it's just that…" I had always wanted to use a dildo with my girlfriends, but none of them were into it. So, as much as I wanted to receive what Lauren wanted to give, there was a stronger urge to fuck her with it instead. Besides, even though I never knew I had it in me to come twice so close together, a third time just seemed like a stretch.

"What is it, darling? You can say whatever it is that you're thinking"—she leaned close to my ear—"or wanting."

I whispered back. "I uh, I actually want to use that on you."

She leaned back and gave me the once-over. "Well, look who's coming out of her shell. If that's what you want…" She extended her arms and I took the dildo and strap. "Then that's what you'll get. Put this on, then you can start by giving me a massage. I think I tweaked my back a bit while I was in that last position." She laughed that cackled laugh as she winked at me.

I hopped off the table and plopped another strawberry in my mouth as I placed the tray on the floor. Lauren disrobed, jumped on, turned on her stomach, and rested her face in the donut at the end of the table. I took the moment and tried to get my bearings with the apparatus. I slipped the dildo in the obvious slot, then stepped into the other two openings. I thought I fastened the clasps tight enough around my thighs and waist, but as soon as I released my grip, the strap fell around my ankles, the dildo hitting the floor with a thud. "Shit," I said as I bent and retrieved the unit.

"Need help?" Lauren said from under her donut.

"No…no. I got it," I said with determination as I wiggled the strap-on up my legs, repositioned it, and tightly tugged on each clasp until this time the dildo pressed firmly against my clit. Oh my, I thought as I adjusted it to the right spot between my legs and nodded at my achievement. I was strapped in and ready to roll.

"There's massage oil in the thing that looks like a cup holder on the left side of the table."

I grabbed the bottle, squirted some in the palm of my hand and smiled at the hint of lavender—my favorite scent—as I rubbed it into my hands. I positioned myself at the side of the table and leaned over her as I pressed my oily fingers into her skin. She moaned in a deep-throated way, and my stomach twitched at the primal sound. I glided my fingers over her shoulders, down to her butt, and around her inner thighs. The closer I got to her clit, the deeper her moan, and I thought how easy it would be to slide a finger over and enter her, but that wasn't the way I wanted to take her.

"Are you enjoying your massage?" I said as I leaned close to her ear.

"Mmm," she moaned. "Very much."

"What do you want?" I decided to turn the tables and ask her the same question she kept peppering me with when the roles were reversed.

"Darling, I'm just the passenger. You're the one who wanted to be in the driver's seat this go-around. So, whatever you have in mind, I suggest you do it soon, because I'm pretty fucking turned on right now."

Several positions flashed through my mind before I settled on the one that seemed to suit the situation the best. "Turn over," I instructed.

She did as I commanded.

"Now scoot down on the table," I said as I grabbed the bottle of oil.

She smiled a knowing smile as she wiggled her body down the table until her legs dangled over the edge. She casually leaned back on bent elbows, and just as I was thinking I might have to stand on my tiptoes to do what I wanted to do to her, she piped up.

"The table is electronic. There are two buttons under the padding. One raises it, the other lowers it," she said as she pointed.

I ran my finger under the right side of the table until I felt the buttons. I pressed one, and the table responded by easing itself down the few inches I needed. I settled myself between her, placed my hands on her thighs, and spread her legs a little wider. I took a step closer to her, and I could tell by her expression that she liked that. She licked her lips, then wrapped her legs around my waist. My slick fingers were still on her thighs, and I could sense from her movement what she wanted. I trailed my one finger over to her slit and ran it up and down. She was so wet, I knew I wouldn't need any lube when it was time to give her what she wanted. What *I* wanted.

She moaned in that way that pleaded for me to go in, and as excited as I was, I held back. This was my fantasy, I was the conductor, and I wanted the crescendo. "Lie down." I placed my hand on her chest and slowly guided her upper body down, until she lay flat on the table. I wanted—no, needed to run my fingers around her body and get to know every inch of the person I was about to make love to. I took a step forward, the tip of the dildo piercing her opening. Her breath caught, but I held my ground. Not yet, I thought, not yet.

I bent and hovered the bottle of oil over her and gave it a little squeeze. Slick liquid dripped from the tip onto her skin. She shuddered with each drop that landed and settled on her flesh. I took my time covering her body, one slow drip at a time, until I thought she was slick enough. I placed the bottle aside and gently pressed my fingers into her chest and began a slow circular motion, rubbing the oil into her skin with each stroke as I slowly inched closer to her bright pink nipples. They were waiting for me to tease them into hardness. I wanted to suck them, but that meant I would have had to scoot closer, and in doing so the dildo would have inserted into her. No, I wanted the tease, so I made sure I was just out of reach as I ran my fingers over her nipples the way I imagined my tongue would, if I was sucking her right now. She closed her eyes, placed her hand over mine, and squeezed. She wanted more pressure on her nipples, and I did as she guided me to do. When I thought they were greased and hard enough, I moved my hands down her abdomen, gathering and dispersing more oil around her body. Her skin felt hot, and I scooped up the last of the drops on my way to her thighs. I rubbed my hands around her legs and down to where the tip of the dildo was perched, waiting to make its entrance. I gently teased my finger up and down the top of her slit as the oil mixed with her wetness. Then I spread her legs just a little more and slowly entered her. She arched her back and moaned deeper as I pushed farther inside her. Her fingers gripped the sides of the table as they searched for something to hold on to as I began to rock my hips.

"Are you okay?" I said as I stopped pulsing.

"Don't hold back," she said in a guttural voice. "I like it fast and hard."

My body released more wetness with those words, as I moved on her, going deeper inside with each thrust. I slid my hands back up to her breasts and pinched her nipples, maintaining the hardness that was there before. Beads of sweat were starting to form again on my skin as I felt the pressure of the dildo against my clit. The harder I moved inside Lauren, the more it pleased me.

I heard the slightest whisper from her lips. I cocked my head and concentrated. "Oh yeah, right there…right there," was what I thought she was saying. I closed my eyes and joined the ride as I tightened my thighs. Between the thrusting, the pressure from the placement of the dildo on me, her voice whispering to me that she was almost there, and her breasts moving back and forth in my hands as they jiggled with the rocking of her body, I was on the verge of exploding again. But I didn't want to come before Lauren did, so I exhaled a breath to steady myself as I glanced down at her. She had her eyes closed, and I knew exactly what she was feeling, because I was just on that end. The feeling of something rubbing inside you, coaxing you to squeeze onto it and feel every movement it makes.

"Yeah, baby," I whispered back as I answered her.

I changed my rhythm and matched her short, sputtered breaths. Now she was setting the pace, and I was just keeping the beat. Her breathing quickened, her voice began to crackle as her words and her moans became inaudible. But I understood what she was telling me, and I moved deeper and faster. The pressure was building in me, and I didn't think I could hold back my release any longer. Just then, she arched her shoulders forward as her thighs squeezed into my waist. I knew she climaxed and was riding out the pulsing, and that thought caused me to release as well. We stayed like that for a moment, each of us silently enjoying our orgasm.

I slowed my thrusting and soon leaned back until I gently guided the dildo out of her. The need to hold her was strong, so I extended my hands. She took them, and I bent forward until we closed the distance in a tight embrace. I didn't know the true identity of my lover, but as I held her tight, I wanted her to know that this evening meant something to me. That *she* meant something to me.

Lauren was the one who broke the embrace, as she leaned back on her locked arms and smiled. After a beat, she reached up and wiped some sweat off my forehead, readjusted my mask, then leaned her head forward and rested it against mine. We stayed like that for a moment, our breaths intertwining, until she leaned out.

"Fuck," was all she said, and I nodded at the sentiment.

I grabbed the robe that was sitting on the floor and opened it for her. She slid her arms in the sleeves, and I wrapped it around her.

I unstrapped and stepped out of the apparatus and held it up. "What should I do with this?"

She hopped off the table, grabbed it, and flung it over her shoulder toward the dresser. It fell short of her mark, but that didn't seem to faze her. "Come this way," she said as she hooked her arm around mine and escorted me over to one of the zero gravity massage chairs. I had been wanting one of these since a salesperson asked me to try it out at the warehouse megastore down the street from my apartment. I eagerly folded myself into the chair and sank deep into the unit. She hit a few buttons on the controls, and the chair responded. It rocked me back as rollers glided over my back and neck.

"I'm going to bring up a tray of real food and a couple glasses of wine. You relax. I'll be right back," she announced.

I nodded, closed my eyes, and gave myself over to a different kind of pleasure. At this point, I no longer asked her if it was okay to use Elizabeth Hathaway's stuff, I just trusted that Lauren knew what she was doing, so I went with it. I heard the distant pitter-patter of her feet, and distant words about reassuring me that she'd be right back as the elevator chimed.

That was the last thing I remembered before everything went black.

❖

I jerked awake and tried to blink in my surroundings. I yawned, reached up to my face, and poked a feather in my eye. "Ouch." I pushed the mask up on my forehead, rubbed my eyes, then glanced around the room. I was still in the massage chair, wrapped in the robe.

"Lauren?" I called out but she was nowhere in sight. "Lauren?" I repeated.

I stretched, replaced my mask, and scooted out of the chair as a piece of paper floated off my body and down to a stack of my clothes that had been neatly folded and placed at the base of the chair. I bent and pinched the paper between my fingers. The note was simple.

Darling, I didn't have the heart to disturb you. I hope you enjoyed your evening and found what you were looking for.

I smiled and took a moment to glance once more around a room that was the backdrop to an evening I would never forget.

"I will miss you, Lauren." I quickly got dressed, said good-bye to the memories, and summoned the elevator. I shoved Lauren's note in my front pocket, entered the empty container, yawned again, and shook out the fatigue that still had a grip on me.

A moment later, I shuffled into the main room of the estate and noticed the guests had really thinned out. A few were lingering, a throuple was having sex on the couch, and others stood in the corner chatting. A staff member rolled a cart past and offered me some coffee.

"Coffee? Wait...what time is it?" I sleepily asked.

"Almost two," she replied.

"Holy shit, you've got to be kidding me? It's two in the morning?" I said as alarm bells began ringing in my head. The interview, I needed that interview!

The woman nodded and asked me again if I'd like some coffee. "No, thank you. But if you'd be so kind as to point out Elizabeth Hathaway. I'd like to thank her for a wonderful evening."

"I believe Elizabeth has retired for the night," she said.

Shit, shit, shit! I scrubbed my fingers through my hair. I blew it. The Michelle devil popped up on my shoulder, yelling and telling me what an idiot I was for blowing my chances at getting an exclusive interview. I know, I know, I grumbled to myself as I flicked the little devil off my shoulder.

"You sure I can't get you anything? You seem a little... agitated," the staff member said.

"No," I groaned. "But thank you anyway."

She nodded and pushed her cart over to the group of stragglers huddled in the corner where they seemed more than happy to take her up on her offer. Still in denial about the time, I hustled outside and glanced around at the once bustling backyard. The pool was empty, the water bowl was covered, and as I jogged to the body painting tent, I could already tell the artists had packed up and left hours ago. "Shit, shit, shit!" I repeated as I spun in a three-sixty. I not only blew my chance at an exclusive, but I blew a chance to move on from *What's Buzzin'*. Michelle was going to have my head, and I couldn't really blame her.

I hunched my shoulders as I let out a defeated breath, bowed my head, and staggered back into the house. I heard someone call out and ask if I wanted to join them. "No, thanks," I said without bothering to look up. I wasn't in the mood. Besides, I had already come a personal best of three times tonight, and a fourth just wasn't in me.

Maybe I *was* getting too old for all of this, I thought as I headed for the front door. How in the hell was I going to explain to Michelle and Sandy that I fell asleep at a sex party? I groaned, because I knew that I would never hear the end of it from either of them and anticipated being the butt of their jokes for quite a while.

Lisa was still standing guard by the lockers, looking way too cheery for two in the morning. She acknowledged me as I approached. "Hope you had a wonderful evening," she said.

"I did, thank you, Lisa." I returned the smile, opened locker twenty-three, and grabbed my phone.

"My pleasure," she replied. "Safe travels on your way home."

I thanked her again, fired up my phone, and walked over to Ruby with my head bent to my screen. "Hey, Ruby," I said as I dug in my pocket and retrieved the ticket. As I handed it to her, I couldn't help lingering one more time at her breasts before she hustled off to retrieve my Jeep. I took the moment to scroll through my text messages. Sandy left five, all wanting to know how the evening went. Michelle left one asking if I got the interview, and Todd left another saying my article was written and posted. Maybe I would buy some donuts and bring them to the office Monday morning to thank him. I shallowed hard. The thought pained me.

I squinted when the lights of my Jeep flashed across my face, and I smiled when Ruby exited my car and held the door for me.

"Thanks, Ruby."

"My pleasure," she said as she backed away.

I hopped in, tossed my phone on the passenger seat, shed my mask, and as I slowly pulled away, I leaned out my open window. "By the way, Ruby…you wear your tux better than any other person that was here this evening."

She called out a thanks as the sensory lights in the road lit and guided me out. According to my Jeep, it was seventy-eight degrees out, which for me was the perfect temperature, and as I slowly meandered down the hill and back to the reality of my life, I rested my arm on the doorframe and let the wind wash over my thoughts. So I didn't get the interview with Elizabeth, so what? The article would still have all the bells and whistles needed to capture the attention of our readers. I'd give Michelle enough of what she wanted, and *What's Buzzin'* would gain followers and advertisers. But still, I was better than that. I should have said no to Lauren and stayed focused. But then again, Lauren gave me the gift of finding something inside me that I never knew was missing.

I decided not to hop on the freeway, but instead took the back streets home. I was wired, not tired, and I had the time to kill. I turned down Las Vegas Boulevard and made my way down the Strip. At this hour, there was still a little movement on the street, but the majority of tourists were either in the casinos or tucked away in their rooms. The fountains were still, the street entertainers were gone, and the hum of the traffic was almost nonexistent.

The neon lights still flashed, blinked, and lit up the darkness, their colors spilling over my windshield as I made my way north on the Strip. Those four-plus miles of enticing eye candy reminded me I was in a city like no other and it was a far cry from the small Missouri farming community I grew up in. If my high school friends could see me now… I chuckled the thought to myself as I drove past the Strat and veered east. The thought of calling Sandy and having her meet me at the local casino by my house crossed my mind. She was a night owl, and more than once we had traded sleep for an all-nighter of gambling. I glanced at my dash, and the time on the digital clock talked me out of it. Nah, it was almost three, and truthfully, the time alone let me replay the highlights of my evening with Lauren.

Thirty minutes later, I pulled into my designated parking spot and walked up the flight of stairs to my humble abode. I opened the door, and the stillness that greeted me was a sober reminder that I really needed another furry friend in my life. I missed coming home to tail wags and kisses.

I emptied my pockets and tossed everything on the coffee table. Lauren's note sat on top of the pile, and as I reread it, I thought about Elizabeth. "No," I said. "I didn't find what I was looking for." Oh well, I saw enough, and since sex sells, I was going to pepper the article with plenty of it.

I ventured into the kitchen, made some tea and a peanut butter and jelly sandwich, and returned to the couch. I flopped down, put my phone on do not disturb, grabbed my laptop, and began writing. I started by painting a descriptive narrative of the estate and then set the mood as I walked the reader through scene after scene of decadent sex. The words flew from my fingertips, and within an hour, I had an article written that would make anyone reading it wet themselves.

I was about to send it off to Michelle when Lauren's note caught the corner of my eye. *Did I find what I was looking for?* I leaned back into the couch cushion and paused as that question stuck in my head. Maybe it wasn't about finding Elizabeth and scoring an exclusive interview. Maybe it was more about finding oneself in an environment, surrounded by other women, that allowed everyone to feel free. Maybe in the end, *that's* what the party was really about.

I minimized the document that I had just written and started another. Only this time, I wrote a piece not just about the salacious side of the party, but instead, about how the event allowed the guests to lose their inhibitions and find a part of themselves that they might have never known before.

By the time I completed the second article, the sun had been up for hours, and I could hear my fellow apartment dwellers going about their day. I yawned, reread both pieces, and debated which of the two to send to Michelle. After a moment, I settled on the one with feelings, hoping that Michelle would appreciate the depth and insight of my writing.

I closed the laptop and pushed myself deeper into the cushion and deeper into thoughts about Lauren. Her smile, her mesmerizing turquoise eyes, and that cackle of a laugh. I wished I had asked for her number. It would be nice to see her again. But maybe that wasn't what it was about for her. Maybe for Lauren, it was only about the anonymous sex and nothing more. The thought made me feel a little lonely, and yet, could I really expect anything more from a masquerade ball called Decadence.

I grabbed the remote, wrapped myself in a thin blanket, and nestled into my favorite well-worn neck pillow. As I flipped through endless channels on the TV, my eyes began to blink less and stay shut more, until the voices on the show faded away and sleep took hold.

I had no idea how long I had been asleep when I startled from the screeching sound of a car alarm. "Mirna." I yawned my eighty-year-old neighbor's name as I stretched. No matter how many times I told her she needed to get out of her car first, then set the alarm, she never seemed to remember. I rolled over and closed my eyes, hoping to fall back to sleep, when my eyes flew open. Mirna always went to her water aerobics class at three. Early that morning I'd texted Sandy that I'd pick her up at her house at four thirty and take her out to dinner. Shit! I hopped off the couch, rubbed at the soreness settling into my neck, tapped my phone, and took it off do not disturb. I ventured into the kitchen to make some coffee as notifications chimed their distinct jingles. I would get to them after a large cup of wake-up juice.

Mug in hand, I flopped back on the couch and began scrolling through my messages. I had thirteen text messages, two emails, and one voice message. I opened my texts and wasn't surprised to see all of them were from Sandy. The girl obviously had issues with patience. After reassuring her that *yes*, we were still on for dinner this evening, and that *yes*, I would tell her all about the Decadence ball, I moved on to my emails. Michelle had sent back my article saying she didn't give two flying fucks about my newfound feelings and epiphanies. She wanted an article riddled with sex, sex, and more sex. I groaned but understood as I fired up my laptop, sent her my other file, and peppered it with smiling emojis and a meme that said I was only joking. I wasn't, but she didn't need to know that.

Finally, I opened my voice mail, hit the speaker icon, and ventured into the kitchen to replenish my cup. I froze halfway there when I heard the sultry voice of Lauren coming through my phone.

"Hello, darling. So sorry I didn't say good-bye last night, but other pressing matters were calling. Anyway, just dropping you a note to let you know you left something behind last night and I was wondering if you wanted to come by this afternoon, say around five, and get it? You know the address."

The voice mail ended and I stood stunned. I hurried back to the coffee table and replayed the message three times. "I left something?" I checked the small pile of items still sitting on the coffee table and did a mental inventory. I had my wallet, phone, keys, Lauren's note, and Sandy's mask was in the car. I glanced at my clothes. Yep, same clothes as yesterday. I even unzipped my jeans to double make sure I had retrieved my underwear. Yep to that too. Hmm, so what the hell did I leave behind? And not only that, how the hell did Lauren get my number?

I played the voice mail one more time, even though I pretty much had it memorized by now. I glanced at the time. Three thirty. Shit! I texted Sandy the change of plans and told her the details I would share when I eventually saw her would more than make up for the rain check. I jumped in the shower and thirty minutes later hustled out the door.

I retrieved the address from my maps app archive and hit the freeway. Forty minutes later—which included a stop at a coffee shop for a cappuccino and muffin and a slice of banana nut bread—I pulled up to the call box and powered down my window. The QR scanner was gone, so I hit the green button. A voice that sounded like Lauren's answered.

"Yes?"

"Hi. This is Addison Miller, I'm here to—"

The click of the gate interrupted me, and just as I did last night, I checked myself in the visor mirror as I waited for the arms to swing open and once again welcome me. The house in daylight was much different than the one last night. I would argue that the magnificence of the fountain and the sheer magnitude of the estate was even more awe-inspiring now that I was able to take in the enormity of the property. I pulled up to the front and parked. Gone were Ruby, Lisa, Shelly, and the lockers. I approached the front door and, without the help of an escort, glanced around for a doorbell. A camera spun and turned on me. I waved and moments later, heard the click of the door unlock. I cautiously walked in. The house was spotlessly cleaned and showed no signs or slightest hint that a masquerade ball even took place here.

"Hard to believe there was a party here at all," the sultry voice announced.

I looked around, then up. Lauren was standing on the balcony dressed in a white robe, glancing down at me. She had on the same shade of red lipstick as she did last night. Her hair was styled a little differently, but the eyes twinkling down at me were undeniable. She was beautiful.

I waved. "Hi. You, um, you said in your message that I left something here last night?"

"Yes. Come on up. Take the elevator," she said as she turned and walked away.

I shuffled to the back corner of the great room, took a moment to locate the button, and summoned the elevator. The doors slid open, and I hopped in. I took the moment to sniff under my armpits and mess with my hair until the doors opened and deposited me in the middle of the bedroom I had left only hours ago. Lauren stood over by the sitting area and my stomach lurched as I remembered her touch. By the time I walked the short distance to her, I was already wet.

"Have a seat." She motioned to a chair, and I did as I was told.

She sat and took a moment as she gave me the once-over. "You're even more stunning without the mask," she said.

I blushed and lowered my eyes as she crossed her legs and cleared her throat.

"So," she said. "Let's get down to business, then let's play. I so enjoyed our time last night, darling." She winked.

I swallowed hard. "Um, business?"

"Yes, you seemed to have left the one thing you couldn't find."

I cocked my head as I blankly stared at her.

"The interview…and, darling, we can't have that." She leaned back in her chair, and as her leg rocked a bit, she strummed her fingers on the armrest. "Well, what are you waiting for? Ask me anything."

I blinked once, then twice. "I knew it." I chuckled as I stabbed a finger at her. "You're Elizabeth."

"It appears as though I am." She laughed that deep-throated laugh that quickly turned into a cackle.

"And you're the one who sent me the invitation, aren't you?"

"Guilty as charged. After you left such pleading messages for me, I looked you up and liked what I saw."

A heat of embarrassment flushed my face as I whipped the phone from my back pocket, set it on the armrest, and began recording. "Well, thank you for the invitation. Last night was amazing, and let me start this interview by stating, on the record, it is a pleasure meeting you, Elizabeth."

"Oh, trust me." She slipped her foot out of her sandal, placed it on my crotch, and pressed her toes into me. "The pleasure is all mine."

About the Authors

RONICA BLACK lives in the metropolitan Phoenix area with her rescue Chiweenie, Frankie. When she's not happily lost in writing or reading, she enjoys drawing, painting, sculpting, and doing anything crafty. She also enjoys hiking Arizona's beautiful trails and discovering new vegan recipes.

RENEE ROMAN lives in upstate New York with her fur baby, Maisie. She is blessed by close friends and a supportive family. She is passionate about many things including living an adventurous life, exploring her authentic self, and writing lesbian romance and erotica.

PIPER JORDAN lives in Southern Arizona with her gang of fur babies. She enjoys sunset hikes, traveling, and spending time with family and friends. Piper also writes sweet romance as Toni Logan.

Books Available From Bold Strokes Books

Crush by Ana Hartnett Reichardt. Josie Sanchez worked for years for the opportunity to create her own wine label, and nothing will stand in her way. Not even Mac, the owner's annoyingly beautiful niece Josie's forced to hire as her harvest intern. (978-1-63679-330-6)

Decadence by Ronica Black, Renee Roman & Piper Jordan. You are cordially invited to Decadence, Las Vegas's most talked about invitation-only Masquerade Ball. Come for the entertainment and stay for the erotic indulgence. We guarantee it'll be a party that lives up to its name. (978-1-63679-361-0)

Gimmicks and Glamour by Lauren Melissa Ellzey. Ashly has learned to hide her Sight, but as she speeds toward high school graduation she must protect the classmates she claims to hate from an evil that no one else sees. (978-1-63679-401-3)

Heart of Stone by Sam Ledel. Princess Keeva Glantor meets Maeve, a gorgon forced to live alone thanks to a decades-old lie, and together the two women battle forces they formerly thought to be good in the hopes of leading lives they can finally call their own. (978-1-63679-407-5)

Peaches and Cream by Georgia Beers. Adley Purcell is living her dreams owning Get the Scoop ice cream shop until national dessert chain Sweet Heaven opens less than two blocks away and Adley has to compete with the far too heavenly Sabrina James. (978-1-63679-412-9)

The Only Fish in the Sea by Angie Williams. Will love overcome years of bitter rivalry for the daughters of two crab fishing families in this queer modern-day spin on Romeo and Juliet? (978-1-63679-444-0)

Wildflower by Cathleen Collins. When a plane crash leaves eleven-year-old Lily Andrews stranded in the vast wilderness of Arkansas, will she be able to overcome the odds and make it back to civilization and the one person who holds the key to her future? (978-1-63679-621-5)

Witch Finder by Sheri Lewis Wohl. Tasmin, the Keeper of the Book of Darkness, is in terrible danger, and as a Witch Finder, Morrigan must protect her and the secrets she guards even if it costs Morrigan her life. (978-1-63679-335-1)

Digging for Heaven by Jenna Jarvis. Litz lives for dragons. Kella lives to kill them. The last thing they expect is to find each other attractive. (978-1-63679-453-2)

Forever's Promise by Missouri Vaun. Wesley Holden migrated west disguised as a man for the hope of a better life and with no designs to take a wife, but Charlotte Rose has other ideas. (978-1-63679-221-7)

Here For You by D. Jackson Leigh. A horse trainer must make a difficult business decision that could save her father's ranch from foreclosure but destroy her chance to win the heart of a feisty barrel racer vying for a spot in the National Rodeo Finals. (978-1-63679-299-6)

I Do, I Don't by Joy Argento. Creator of the romance algorithm, Nicole Hart doesn't expect to be starring in her own reality TV dating show, and falling for the show's executive producer Annie Jackson could ruin everything. (978-1-63679-420-4)

It's All in the Details by Dena Blake. Makeup artist Lane Donnelly and wedding planner Helen Trent can't stand each other, but they must set aside their differences to ensure Darcy gets the wedding of her dreams, and make a few of their own dreams come true. (978-1-63679-430-3)

Marigold by Melissa Brayden. Marigold Lavender vows to take down Alexis Wakefield, the harsh food critic who blasts her younger sister's restaurant. If only she wasn't as sexy as she is mean. (978-1-63679-436-5)

A Second Chance at Life by Genevieve McCluer. Vampires Dinah and Rachel reconnect, but a string of vampire killings begin and evidence seems to be pointing at Dinah. They must prove her innocence while finding out if the two of them are still compatible after all these years. (978-1-63679-459-4)

The Town That Built Us by Jesse J. Thoma. When her father dies, Grace Cook returns to her hometown and tries to avoid Bonnie Whitlock, the woman who pulverized her heart, only to discover her father's estate has been left to them jointly. (978-1-63679-439-6)